IRKADURA

Dear Reader,
this is a scary
story scraped off
the snowy Moscow
streets...
xoxo
Ksenia Anske

IRKADURA

KSENIA ANSKE

ISBN-13: 978-1503040113
ISBN 10: 1503040119

For Michael Gruber, who asked me to write this

CONTENTS

CHAPTER ONE

MOUSE

I wake up and feel for the boar. The boar is Lyosha Kabansky, mama's boyfriend. He's there all right, snoring. It's September first. I don't need to go to school anymore and I could've slept in, but I'm leaving. He tried to sell me yesterday. He said, "Irkadura, this is Vova. You know what to do. I'll give you a ruble for some ice cream." I wouldn't do it, so he beat me. Then they had me. They took turns, Lyosha and Vova. Drunk.

I turned into a mouse to escape them. It's easier that way.

I'm sixteen and I'm mute.

It's good you have a fat dick, Lyosha. Something for me to hold on to, when I gut you.

It's like he heard me. He grunts and turns to mama.

My mama is a catfish. She sleeps by Lyosha's other side,

filthy, fat, and naked. She became a catfish when I was two, on the day I stopped talking.

I was sitting on a potty and I learned how to say my first word, dura. I waddled up to mama and I said, "Dua." I couldn't roll the r.

She kept her eyes closed. "Be quiet."

I watched the curtains sway, the maroon curtains over the balcony window. The rotting parquet pissed through by cats and dogs. "Dua," I said, so happy I could say it. "Dua, dua."

She said, "Go away."

I touched her shoulder.

"What?" She sat up. "What do you want?"

"Dua."

"Who's dura? Irka, who taught you this, huh?" Her face was crumpled with pillow creases. "You dumb girl. I'll show you dura." She struck me.

I flew to the potty and knocked it over. My urine soaked into my shirt and wet my face. She beat me. When I looked up, my mama was gone. In her place was a catfish. A big, scary catfish. It hung over me with its open suckermouth and it breathed its stagnant stink into my face. It hurt me. I bit my tongue lying on the floor by the curtains, right by the maroon curtains.

I never said another word.

Lyosha snorts, opens one eye.

I freeze.

"Where you going?"

Where pigs like you get quartered.

He mumbles something and drops back to sleep.

He showed up at our door last year with red carnations in one hand and a bottle of Stolichnaya in the other. A discharged butcher after three years in prison. I knew he was a boar right away, from the greedy glint in his eyes.

On the very first night he got mama drunk and he did me for the first time and every night after that. I was not a virgin and it made him disappointed and angry. He slapped me. There were scores before him, stray dogs my mama picked up from the dingy Moscow streets. Grubby men without money who liked to use my parts.

I pinch myself. *Go, you dimwit. Get out.*

I think about everything I hate.

Lenochka's taunting and explosive laughter. Auntie Sonya's jokes. Cat smell, mites in bed, soiled bedding on the floor. Dog sex under the kitchen table. Grandma drowning newborn puppies in the bucket. Piles and piles of dirty dishes in the kitchen sink. And the shouting about who'd be washing them, the yelling and the screaming and the fighting and the pulling of hair.

I dress quietly, steal five rubles from mama's stash under an empty vodka bottle, stuff my backpack with a change of clothes, and tiptoe to the corridor. I know all the planks that don't creak. I click the front door shut, skid down eighteen flights of stairs, and step out into the open, into yellow leaves and wind.

"Irkadura!"

I crane my neck. Grandma is waving at me from the ninth-floor window of our Brezhnevka faced with bleached tile and streaked with mold. "Where are you off to? It's seven in the morning! You don't need to go to school anymore!" She is the

3

cockroach.

Auntie Sonya leans out, the big herring. "Irkadura! Get back! Take the dogs out!"

Lenochka squeezes in below, the little herring. "Irkadura lost her mind! Irkadura lost her mind! Irkadura—"

Sonya slaps her. "Quiet. People are looking."

Lenochka wails.

"Irka, wait!"

I run without looking and bump into a boy in a navy uniform with a little Octobrist star on his lapel. He holds a bouquet of asters. His mother says to me, "Watch where you're going."

I bolt down the long apartment block, with its grimy porches and rows of snowberry bushes sprinkled with white berries that I like to pop. I round the corner and pass the grocery store, and the ice cream kiosk that sells coffee gum, my favorite flavor. The sports store with bicycles on display, Kama and Salut. I want a Salut but it costs one hundred rubles and nobody in my family can afford it.

I stop in the small public garden by my school, number 318. It's framed in chestnut trees. In the center of the asphalt square begonia flowerbeds surround a life-sized statue of Lenin. His one arm is pointed at the bright proletariat future and the other clutches his coat's lapel. His eyes are dead and splotched with bird poop.

I kick at the chestnut shells. Some are cracked with shiny kernels inside. I pick one up, peel it, and throw it at a flock of pigeons. They scatter.

Festive children and their parents begin to arrive at the square for the first school day. Boys in uniform navy suits and girls in white lacy aprons over brown dresses, their braids tied with ribbons, led by their mamas and papas and grandmas.

I gather a handful of chestnuts and aim at one girl. She looks about eight, plump and smiley, her hand held by a modish, lipsticked mama.

Too bad these aren't stones to take out your smile.

I throw and miss her by a meter, gather more.

Why are you so happy? What did you eat for breakfast, caviar? Did you fry your fat little tummy all summer in the hot Krymsky sun?

"Citizen Myshko."

I whirl around.

The statue of Lenin is talking to me. "Come, citizen. I have an important question to ask you. What is your goal in life?"

I have no life.

"You don't know? Ay-ay, that's not good. I will tell you. Your goal in life is to devote yourself to the Soviet state and to become a Bolshevik."

The chestnuts drop from my hand.

Lenin shakes a finger at me. "Who is a Bolshevik? A Bolshevik is the one who leads our revolutionary work." He rolls his *r* in a strange, crippled way. "You know what work I'm speaking of, Myshko?" A thunderous step off the pedestal, smashed begonias under his boots.

My palms are sweaty. I back up, into a bench.

"No, I see that you do not. That's a shame. Ten school years and all of them wasted. You, citizen Myshko, are of the Menshevik faction. I can see it." Another step. "You're a mouse, a selfish vermin. A criminal."

I can't move.

"Your crime is that you don't understand the essence of the Soviet power."

Pioneers in red neckerchiefs detach from the school crowd and come to his aid.

"Are you ready?" he asks them.

"Always ready!" they say, and change into giant woodpeckers with small, hungry eyes. They peck at me.

"You forgot your neckerchief again!"

"You didn't iron it!"

"You'll be banned from the Pioneer Organization!"

I cower.

"Do you know what happens to bad pioneers, citizen Myshko?" says Lenin. "To those pioneers who refuse to join the communist revolution?"

They turn into deranged maniacs, their heads stuffed with your bogus equality theories.

"Their necks get snapped like this." Lenin grabs a woodpecker and flips it around. A bone crunches, wings flap spasmodically and hang limp. He throws the dead woodpecker at my feet. "This is what happens to those who don't believe in the Soviet power. The Soviet power will triumph all over the world!" The second woodpecker is cracked in a blur. "Necessarily!" The third. "Inevitably!" The fourth. "Permanently!"

I believe in my ass, because your government is shit. Your propaganda is lies. I'd rather die than fit your ideals.

I whack the statue across the face with my backpack. It topples over and lands in a cloud of dust. The woodpeckers screech and disband.

I run under the arch between two conjoined dismal apartment blocks, cross a broken playground, and emerge by the line of buses and trolleybuses at the Belyaevo metro station where I join the sweaty mob squeezing through the flapping glass doors. Nausea seizes my gut. My mouth tastes sour. I pass by the booth attendant yelling at a pensioner for an outdated permit, press both thumbs into the turnstile barriers, and skip without paying.

"Hey! Stop! Militia!"

I ford a noisy platform thick with people. Marble columns, steel panels embossed with fairy tale birds. I halt on the very edge and watch the train emerge from the tunnel as if from the bowels of Moscow metro. It crawls along the tracks like a green tapeworm with five eyes and eight body segments.

The sliding doors open. Eager bodies push me inside. There is no space to stand freely and no air to breathe. More people press from the platform. A squabble breaks out.

"Let go of the doors," says the machinist's voice over the intercom.

I grip the handrail and hang over those who managed to sit down. The next station is announced and the doors slam shut. The train lurches to a measured staccato of wheels. Bodies shift with it, their bad breath, their unwashed skin odor, yellowing teeth, and dull eyes.

A hand lands on my buttock.

I stiffen.

You pervert.

There is no room for me to turn and my vision swims from an urge to retch. I swallow to keep it down, squint. The train car walls wilt to the color of rotten yolk. Lights dim. A drop of warm sweat rolls down my back under my shirt and I know it's coming. The air around me folds with a squelch and I shrink and—

The mouse sits on the gritty floor in a narrow gap between endless shoes. It squeals. It's afraid. It feels a long and slimy thing sloshing inside it, the thing that came from the boar. It sprung out and uncoiled and lodged itself in the mouse's belly and latched onto its gut. The mouse taps a frantic dance. When the train stops, it hurries out, dodging stomping feet.

I'm back to myself, and I blink and press my head on the cool marble column. Bright light shines in my eyes. Stale metro warmth clings to my skin. The hum of commuters and trains coming and going. A solicitous face asks, "Are you all right?" A pat on the shoulder. I nod. I have almost fainted. This is not good. That dreadful thought is back at me again. I don't want it, but it stays. It nags at me with annoying repetition.

I'm pregnant.

Despite the lemon wedge, despite the potassium permanganate.

I lift my sweater and grab a handful of skin and twist it until it hurts.

You deserve this, dura. You deserve this.

My diaphragm pushes up sour bile and I don't know how I don't throw up. I heave, swallow, wipe my mouth with the back of my hand, and walk to the center of the vestibule and tilt my head up.

The indicator board says it's the Teatralnaya station.

CHAPTER TWO

TURTLE

I halt at the top of the underpass stairs and grip the handrail to stop the swaying. The avenue is congested with traffic. Hysterical crowing rises from the middle of the Theatre Square by the two-ton granite statue of Karl Marx. Roosters congregate around it, shaking their combs and wattles and red flags in clamor and outrage. A cock climbs onto a platform and cries into a megaphone short phrases that bound off the walls. "We demand!" and "Hold dear the fate of Russia!" and "For Stalin!"

I venture along the sidewalk against the flow of the onlookers. The light turns green and I cross the street, walking away from this farce and rounding the corner into a quiet bedroom neighborhood.

After a while I stop by a Stalinist apartment block and walk under its archway into an inner court. Something about it feels calm and enticing. Four buildings form a stone sack with countless windows ten stories high. The alleyways are planted with poplars and overgrown maples. In the shadow at the deep end of the yard there is a two-story mansion the color of eggshells. A peeling colonnade runs across its porch, and two heavy doors with gilded handles display posters in their windows.

THE CHAMBER THEATER is printed on the sign.

The theater is surrounded by a low wrought-iron fence. I open the rusty gate and walk through, coming upon the side entrance with its own small separate courtyard hedged off by snowberry bushes. Three benches stand by a broken fountain choked with decaying leaves. I pick a cluster of berries, drop them on the ground, and pop them with my foot, leaving shiny smears on the asphalt.

An expensive-looking car rolls up to the gate and parks. A Mercedes. The man who gets out from the driver's side is about twenty years old and tall and blond and effeminate in his movements. His passenger is younger and shorter and wirier and his hair is dark.

The blond one is a macaw, the long-tailed parrot, I decide, *for his blue coat and his golden hair. And the other one is a butterfly, a black admiral, black like the black silk of his hair.*

They glance at me and through me and over me as if I'm a fixture or a stone statue, and hop up the stairs and disappear inside.

My heart beats fast and loud.

Oh, you sentimental romantic, Irina Myshko. Haven't you seen actors before?

But my feet don't listen and carry me up the steps into the gloom of the theater's foyer. A worn marble staircase runs up and down from the landing. On the wall to the right hangs a bulletin board pinned with announcements so old their paper has turned yellow. To the left is a glass partition and behind it is a small room where a woman is hunched over a desk. She is in her fifties or even sixties; her shoulders are wrapped in a fuzzy shawl, and her button nose supports a pair of oversized glasses.

A turtle, I think. *A Russian tortoise.*

The phone rings and she picks it up.

"Chamber Theater. Ah, Tanechka! No, he's not here yet, but he's coming soon, you hear me?" She passes the receiver to her other hand. "You know Sim, he never says the time." She taps a pen on an open ledger. "Pavlik and Kostya just got here, so you better hurry."

I make my way to her. She hears me and raises her questioning eyes, still listening to the receiver.

I notice a paper taped to the glass.

CLEANING WOMAN NEEDED.

She hangs up the phone and peers at me, her wrinkled neck outstretched.

I unzip my backpack, take out my pad, and write and tear off the page, sliding it into the receiving slot. She doesn't even look at it, flicks it back at me.

"What's this for? I don't need this."

I go through my pantomime.

"Ah, you're one of those. I got you." She waves me away. "Well, I have nothing for you, you hear me? Go away. I don't need your trinkets. This is a theater, not a market. Seryozha!" she calls to the lower stairs.

I push the paper back in.

She sucks in air. "What do you think this is, a game? I told you to get out, devil take you. The lot of you begging around, needy canailles. Seryozha! Where the devil is he when I need him."

She plops into her chair and dials a number.

"Vladimir Kuzmich? It's Faina Ilinichna. I have a deaf-mute here, yes. Seryozha has gone somewhere and I need her escorted out. Could you...yes. Thank you." She puts down the receiver and scribbles something in her ledger.

I slide the page through again. It floats onto her desk.

"I said I don't need this." She scans it and her face smoothens. "Ah, you're for the job? Why didn't you tell me right away?"

I bit off my tongue, metaphorically speaking.

"Well, we can't employ you if you're deaf."

I slide in my disability certificate.

"Myshko, Irina Anatolievna, mute, invalid since the age of two. Goodness gracious." She looks up. "You can't talk at all? No? Why, that's awful. And I, the old dura, thought you're one of those, from the train terminal, devil take me." She opens the door. "Well, come in then. Want some tea?"

I trod inside.

The room is like a tiny closet.

"Here, sit."

She points me to the round table in the corner covered with a red-and-white checkered oilcloth. On top of it are an electric kettle, a china teapot, a box of loose Indian tea, cups, saucers, and an opened packet of shortbread cookies. I lower myself onto a rickety stool.

"There you go."

She starts the water.

"Look at your blue eyes, like my Allochka's."

Grief clouds her face and crumps it.

"Allochka is my daughter. Was my daughter. She died last year in a car crash. It's all Sashka, that alcoholic, devil take him.

12

I told her, I said, don't you mingle with that filth. Do you think she listened? No, never. Stubborn like her father."

She blows her nose into a kerchief, pours me tea.

I sit still, afraid to break the spell.

"He rode it right into a tree and she died instantly. When they told me on the phone, I thought I heard them wrong. I thought, it can't be my Allochka, it just can't. She's too young to die." She sniffs and wipes a tear off her cheek and props up her glasses. "Look at you, so young. One day you'll be a mother. God forbid you outlive your children, you hear me? God forbid! It's better to die together. I'm too much of a coward to follow my Allochka, too much of a coward."

Suddenly, she's livid.

"And that scoundrel Sashka? You know what happened to him? He walked. They let him walk. Brezhnev would've put him in jail right away." She leans over the table. I can see the black hairs of her thin mustache.

"The times we live in, look what is happening. They spit on the law. They're all corrupt." She slaps the table with the flat of her palm. "Every day I watch the news and every day someone is killed. Every day. The crime rates are up, the prices are up. I can't buy a loaf of bread for twenty kopecks like I used to, and my salary is still the same. What should I do, starve myself? Beg on the street? Tell me."

I shrug.

"Be good to Vladimir Kuzmich if he hires you. You look like a decent, honest girl, not like that whore Lida. Lazy woman, never did a good job, not once. Then she got knocked up by some scum and that was that. Don't look at them, eat them."

I sip tea, take a cookie, and don't notice how I eat half of the packet. It's my breakfast.

The door opens and horror steals over me.

The sharp nose, and the beer girdle buttoned up in a gray jacket, and the crumpled pants, and what's inside the pants.

Vova, Lyosha's drinking friend from yesterday.

The jackal.

He recognizes me at once. He rubs his hands and his lips stretch in a sneer full of smugness. "Is this your beggar then, Ilinichna?"

I hold his gaze. *I'll stretch your nose down to your stomach and pop it like a balloon.*

"Ah, Vladimir Kuzmich!" Faina labors up. "Never mind that now. I bothered you for nothing. She's for the job."

"Is she?" He studies me. "Shakalov, Vladimir Kuzmich, theater manager." He stretches out his hand.

I can't bring myself to touch it. There it hangs in front of me, dry skin, whispering bones, and overgrown nails.

"Get up," says Ilinichna to me. "She's mute."

"I know."

"You know?"

"Yes."

I feel his slimy stare on my skin and I lean and take hold of his hand and crush it. But he is stronger and he grinds mine and I wince from pain.

"We've met before, haven't we?" He clicks his tongue. "This should work out really well, Ilinichna, thank you. No whining, no complaining. I like that. My father used to say, silence is a virtue. We'll give it a try, see how you do, and then we can talk about payment."

The word lodges in my gut like a stone. When he did me, he raved that it was my payment for disobedience.

"We have a big performance tonight. You understand what that means, don't you? Important people will be here. Everything has to be tip-top. You will sweep and mop the stage

14

and the auditorium and be done by six o'clock. Understand?"

I fight the mouse inside me.

"Come, I'll show you around."

He drags me out and I'm close to losing it.

His ears shoot up, wool sprouts on his chin and cheeks and creeps up his forehead. His limbs fold and his nails curl and blacken. The steps under my feet crumble to dirt and walls bend into a narrow cavern reeking of animal feces. Roots snatch at my hair and grit fills my eyes and mouth and it smells of damp earth.

Not now, please, not now.

Debilitating numbness grips me.

He puts his hand on my breast. "Easy now. Don't waste your energy for nothing. I'm being nice to you, I'm giving you a job. It's very simple. You know how to please me, don't you? Please me and keep quiet, dura." His claw is up my shirt and another one is down my pants and then both of them are on my throat—

The mouse squeals. The jackal flips it up and catches it between its jaws and tosses it around, playing. The mouse scurries away. A paw smacks it and nudges it back and, tired of the game, the jackal makes its predatory move. Sharp crooked teeth sink into the mouse and it peeps in fright but it doesn't get eaten. It gets chewed and masticated and spit out, alive, for another go, another game.

I'm sprawled on a cold tile floor in some utility room shrouded in dim, hazy light. A cracked sink. A tangle of pipes covered with spider webs, old aluminum buckets, broomsticks, a ladder. It smells of wet rags and mold. I hold on to the wall and pull myself and stand in semi-darkness.

The jackal for the boar, Irina Myshko? Nice exchange.

I trudge to the door and peek out.

A long corridor of beige walls and wooden doors. Warped linoleum on the floor and clumsily patched fissures in the walls and nothing else. No recollection in my mind on how I got here.

I hear voices.

CHAPTER THREE

PARROTS

"Shouldn't we rehearse?" says the first voice, male, low, and deep. Something in it makes me shiver. I step back into the room and leave a crack open to listen. The sound of footsteps is moving in my direction. "I want to practice alone today, Pavlik, I hope you don't mind." This one is male, yet somewhat feminine and nasal, and the vowels are long and drawn out. "I'm sorry, I just need to be alone."

I see them.

The actors, the macaw and the butterfly.

"It's nothing personal, okay?" says the blond one. I glimpse his face, angular and avian and exotic.

They stop directly across from me, a couple of meters away.

I hold my breath.

"Kostya, please," says Pavlik. His profile is soft, his lips are full and twitching. "Is it because—"

"No. Stop it. It's not. I already told you."

I close my eyes and stand still, afraid they'll turn their heads and see my shadow or hear my heartbeat. A jingle of keys and I look out and see them each enter their own dressing room, doors side by side.

I shake my head. *This is bad, Irina Myshko. All you're missing right now is falling for an actor.*

I tiptoe to Pavlik's door.

Stop this nonsense, get to work.

Instead, I read his name printed on a piece of paper that's stuck in a clear plastic slot: BABOCH PAVEL ANTONOVICH, ACTOR.

And on the door next to it: ARAEV KONSTANTIN MIKHAILOVICH, ACTOR.

Pavel.

I roll the name silently on my tongue. It has a nice feel to it. My face burns. I like his proud poise and his polite, unhurried manner of speaking. I press my ear to his door and hear him hum a pleasant tune, his feet swishing on the floor in a slow waltz.

My pulse races. I wonder what it feels like to stand onstage flooded with lights and say beautiful words and make people laugh or cry.

He stops dancing, walks to the door.

I dart into the closet and grab the broom from the corner. I peek out the door and see no one, so I run, retracing the actors' steps up the stairs and along a hallway and, suddenly, I stumble into a large and dark space—the chamber theater performance hall, filled with rows of chairs and the particles of dust in my wake and the weak light from the doorway. An enormous crystal chandelier twinkles dully in the middle of a tall ceiling.

I creep forward row by row and come to the stage, gazing at the gilded beams and rods interlocked into a human-size birdcage. I start sweeping, then pause, the broom hovering above the floor, my eyes fixed on nothing. I wonder if Pavlik's hair is as soft and velvety as butterfly wings.

Cut this foolishness, Irina Myshko, you're ugly.

I get lost in work and the mechanical repetition, and after a while, I stare at the pile of sweepings. I forgot to look for a dustpan. I lean the broom on the wall and run out, turn a corner, and crash into him.

Pavlik.

He is surprised. His face is painted with full stage makeup and it appears insectile and severe because of the sharp contrast of the chalky foundation and the dark eye shadow. He is dressed in a tight black leotard and a pair of big black wings protrude from his back.

"I'm sorry," he says. "I didn't see you coming."

I stare. I know that if I stare any longer I will be a lost cause, and I am, and nothing can tear me away.

"I'm Pavel." He offers his hand. "Pavel Baboch."

I rush around him.

"Where are you going?"

I dodge a flock of actors costumed as exotic birds. Cockatiels, popinjays, lories. All kinds of parrots. They giggle on their way to the performance hall, a faint smell of perfume and powder and smoke on them. I skip down the steps to the end of the corridor and slam into the closet door and bend over and pant, my lungs on fire. Somehow I have found my way.

Pavlik's face hangs in the semi-darkness like an afterimage and it makes me ache.

It's no use trying to catch a butterfly. You either chase it like an idiot for hours only for it to flitter off the moment you think you've got it, or you do catch it and crumple its wings in your sweaty fist and it dies in your hand.

I take a deep breath, find a dustpan, and walk back with my head down.

About ten actors and actresses crowd the cage, hanging off it or climbing it or leaning on it to chat. They all wear skin-tight leotards and fake wings, their faces painted violet, bright green, turquoise, magenta, red. I single out Kostya by his shiny golden hair and his tall lithe frame in blue. Blue and gold. Pavlik says something to him, and they laugh.

I scoop up the trash and carry it to the bin in the hallway. My hands shake. I walk back to the closet, fish out a stiff rag from under the sink, and soften it in hot water. I fill up one of the aluminum buckets and drape the wrung-out rag over the broom and slug back.

I begin to mop.

Calls onstage, laughter.

A hand taps my shoulder. "I'm sorry to bother you."

I flinch.

Pavlik tears his hand away. "I wanted to apologize for scaring you in the hallway."

Scaring me? It's so ludicrous that I smile.

"Yeah, I know. They look stupid." He touches his wings. "It's for tonight's premiere. Are you staying to watch?"

Premiere?

"Is something wrong?"

Kostya saunters up. He's chewing gum. "Who are you talking to?"

"Our new janitor, I think."

The words are on my tongue. *Irina, nice to meet you.* As always, they break at my teeth and dissolve.

"Are you okay?"

"What's your name?" Kostya blows a bubble and pops it. "Do you know her name?"

I go through my pantomime.

"You can't talk?" asks Kostya. "Are you deaf, too?"

"Kostya."

"What? Just calling things by their name. Artists must speak the truth, Pavlik, therein lies our supremacy over ordinary peasants." A bubble bursts and a white film of gum plasters over his lips.

I'd love to see you shot, I think. *Peasants.*

"I'm sorry," says Pavlik.

A volley of handclaps makes us turn and look.

"Good morning, children!" From the gloom of the back row emerges a tall, corpulent man. A seal. Shrewd eyes. Glossy, cleanly shaved face. Hands in the pockets of an expensive suit. A mauve scarf around his neck, ends flung over his broad meaty shoulders.

"Good morning, Sim!"

"Morning!"

Kostya strolls up and lightly pecks the man on each cheek. Actors hop off the stage and swarm him.

"Enough." He shakes them off, although his eyes dance with delight at the attention. "Continue."

They climb back onstage.

"What's with the sour faces? Wake up!" He claps. The sound echoes off the ceiling. His voice fills the auditorium. "Pavlik is first. Kostya, you're next. Tanechka, what happened to your face?"

"What?" Tanechka, a red lory, feels her cheeks.

"Why is it bloated? Go do a cold compress. Back onstage in ten. Go!" He claps and she's off.

"Who are you?"

I don't feel my legs.

"Who is this? Someone tell me, she seems to have swallowed her tongue."

Pavlik whispers in his ear.

"She is? That's unfortunate."

Pavlik says something else.

"I'll ask Shakalov. I'm sorry, my child, I didn't know. My name is Kotik, Simeon Ignatievich. Sim for short. I'm the theater director. You must be our new janitor?"

I nod.

"I understand that you're doing your job, but I need you to leave. We're starting our rehearsal." He pins me with his gaze, as if he can see right through me.

I can't bear it. I spin and flee, mop and bucket aloft.

I'll come back to watch you play, Pavlik.

I scrub and wash and clean and I'm done an hour before six. I buy an Olivier salad in the cafeteria and eat it, washing it down with a hot tea with sugar while I wait. The theater shimmers with excited silence before the performance. The cafeteria is empty, save for the bored serving girl. I put the plate in the metal tray for dirty dishes and make my way to the vestibule to spy on the spectators standing in line. I draw back the heavy velvet curtain and watch them through the glass streaked with rain. It pounds on the rooftops of their umbrellas, glistening in the streetlight.

Ushers' footfalls and voices come from around the corner.

A moment of panic, and I dart along the hall and through the doorway before they see me; I hide behind a drape by the doorway nearest the stage and peek out. Musicians enter the orchestra pit, move chairs, sit and tune their cellos and violins, and test the piano.

The din of the crowd takes over the ushers' cries.

"Tickets! Tickets! Show your tickets!"

The public streams in and, in minutes, the place is packed. Every seat is taken. People stand on the carpeted steps between row sections and lean over gilded balcony edges, shouting. I sneak out from behind the curtain and mingle in.

The chandelier dims. Darkness quiets the noise. The stage lights throw pillars of green, blue, and yellow on the red curtains. Everything grows still and, for a few seconds, there is not a sound. Then a cough breaks the tension and, as if by an unspoken signal, the hall burst into applause. It grows, crests, and dies. The conductor mounts the podium and lifts his baton. The orchestra begins playing light, playful music.

I stand on my toes to see better over the three rows of heads in front of me.

The curtains part. Kostya prances out. He is dazzlingly blue. His gestures are comical and exaggerated and bird-like. He jiggles and hops and skips and spreads his arms like wings to the music without words. One by one, more parrots strut out. Pavlik is last, a mote of black amidst color. They crowd him and tousle him and force him into the cage. Kostya speaks in verses, but I don't hear him. I'm on the edge. I know it's a play and I shouldn't worry, and yet I can't help it. The way they toss their heads and aim at him as if to kill him.

My heart is in my throat and—

The mouse doesn't see the birds from the floor but it hears them, the flapping of their wings and the scratching of their claws and their hungry squawks. They attack the butterfly. They screech at it and hammer it. The mouse scurries to the stairs that lead onstage. It's dark and stuffy and hot. It can't find its way; it circles aimlessly and jitters and jumps, startled by the sound of hundreds of clapping hands.

The applause brings me back.

"Bravo!"

"Encore!"

"Kotik! Kotik!"

With his arms open in welcome, Sim strolls out and joins hands with the actors as they stretch into a line and bow. They blow kisses, retreat, grab hands and bow again, and again. Finally, they don't return. The curtains close. The musicians begin to pack their instruments and leave, and the spectators file out in a babbling stream.

I walk to the empty orchestra pit and turn around to look behind me. I'm alone.

You're a mouse, Irina Myshko, a puny creature. You spent your life hiding in a hole and you stink of rodent droppings. Where do you think you're going?

I climb onstage.

CHAPTER FOUR

JACKAL

My heart is in my mouth. I no longer know how to stand. I stare out at the performance hall. Rows and rows and rows of scarlet velvet seats, gilded balconies, and the chandelier. I touch the cage. The bars are cool and smooth. I clutch them and climb up, perching on the top like a bird. The air dampens, grows cold. I smell mold and decay and animal stink.

I'm not alone anymore.

In the center of the front row sits the boar. Next to it reclines the catfish. They stifle yawns. The giant cockroach scurries up and drops by the boar's feet like a dog. Two herrings slither in and twist into a seat.

"Whatcha looking at? Go ahead. Show us what you can do," says the boar.

"What are you doing sitting on that thing for, huh?" says the catfish. "You'll fall and break your neck, dura."

"You've got to be joking me. A mouse can't act," says the herring. "A mouse is good for one thing only."

"What's that?" says the little herring.

"For food, you idiot. To be fed to a boar or to a jackal or some such."

"Irka onstage. Can you believe it?" says the cockroach.

Get out of here.

They turn up their heads.

I want you out.

They laugh and the sound of their laughter swells and fills the hall with cackle and rouse and beasts of every kind. The woodpeckers and the roosters and the tapeworm and the turtle and the many colorful parrots and the jackal in the shadows—

The mouse clings to the cage. The sea in front of it is beaks and teeth and hooves and fins and claws. They roar and snarl and crawl toward it. And then they see the butterfly. It flitters up and over them but it doesn't reach the mouse. The jackal jumps and clamps it in its jaws. The mouse loses its grip, plummets down. The mob is upon it, biting, stinging, jabbing. The howl of the jackal makes them part to let it through.

I squint to make out the face above me.

"Get up," says Shakalov. "We're going to my office."

I'm sprawled on the floor inside the cage. The back of my head hurts as if from a heavy blow. I pull myself upright and follow Shakalov on unsteady legs. My hands shake. My stomach feels nauseous again. I sense being watched, turn around. In the door stands Sim Kotik with his arms crossed and his face contorted in dislike. For a second we stare at each other, then he breaks the gaze and walks away.

Two deserted hallways, one staircase down and one up. We stand in front of a shabby door at the end of a dark corridor. Same printed piece of paper stuck in the same plastic slot.

SHAKALOV VLADIMIR KUZMICH, THEATER MANAGER.

He procures a set of keys and, suddenly, I know what's coming but I'm too weak to resist. All I want is rest. My abdomen cramps and I try not to imagine the thing that sits inside me, and in a strange way, hope that maybe this will cause a miscarriage.

Shakalov pushes me in, locks the door, and turns on the light.

His office is a small drab room with a single window that overlooks the backyard fountain and the yellowing maples, dark and wet in the evening rain. A sooty lampshade on an institutional desk of fake oak. A frayed rug, a couple armchairs by a lopsided coffee table, and above it on the wall, four portraits in dusty wooden frames: Lenin, Karl Marx, Engels, and a balding, mustached man I don't recognize against a red background with a swastika-like symbol.

They grin in a lewd way as if all they want is for him to do me—and he does. Right on the filthy carpet, right in front of their eyes. I can't even lift my arms to push him off. My only hope is that I won't puke all over myself and won't descend into a mouse.

Stay present, Irina Myshko. Don't let it take you.

My blood boils and my breath comes in rattles. The taste

in my mouth is sour and a small proud smile touches my lips.

"Good girl," he says. "Please me and you'll get your payment."

He pants. It's hard for him to come.

You know what I'm going to do with that money? I'll buy a syringe and fill it with eggs and spritz them into the seat of your ratty car and after a week it will stink so badly between your legs you'll think your dick has rotted.

"Get up." He zips up his pants. "Here." He gives me a five ruble banknote.

What a step up from one ruble fare. I don't have to share with my pimp, I can retain one hundred percent of the profits. I pocket it, fix my clothes, and smooth my hair.

"Lyosha is looking for you. You ran away, didn't you?"

I hope your liver bursts.

"Be a good girl and I won't tell him you're here. You can stay in the theater, sleep in a spare dressing room."

I hope one day to see both of you dead. It will make me happy.

"You're lucky because I like you. Silence makes things easier, don't you think?"

Little do you know.

He gives me a brass key, then shoves me out the door and locks it. I look at the number scratched on the head and meander through the poorly lit corridors until I find the room at the end of the hall next to the utility closet. I enter the musty darkness, slump on the pile of costumes in the corner, and cry myself to sleep.

It's October.

In the mornings I clean, then watch rehearsals from the back of the auditorium, eat in the canteen; in the evenings, I sneak into the shows without paying. Shakalov uses me a couple times a week in the utility closet or in his office or in the spare dressing room where I sleep after all theater personnel have left the building. I live off of what Ilinichna feeds me, and I fail to buy eggs and a syringe using the money for food instead. I drop dead tired to sleep every night and wake up early to pick up the broom and the mop and set out to work.

The cracked clock on the wall shows six a.m. The air in the room is frigid. I sneeze, fling off a moth-eaten blanket, and sit up on the thin mattress. There are no windows here, but stacks and stacks of cardboard boxes stuffed with stage props, wigs, and masks. An empty vanity table and several racks of costumes.

I dress, hobble to the utility room, wash my face over the sink with cold rusty water, and wipe under my arms and between my legs. I haven't had a shower in over a month and there isn't one in the theater.

What have I become?

I brush my hair with my fingers and go to Pavlik's dressing room. I have the key to clean it but I come here every morning before the theater opens to look at his things, to touch them and to smell them and to imagine.

I turn on the light and shut the door. Two hours to myself. One and a half to be safe.

This is so stupid.

I sit in front of his mirror at his makeup table and feel somehow at home amidst all this. Mannequin heads in wigs. An old sofa. A coffee table. A wheeled rack of costumes. Costumes on the hangers, on the hooks on the wall, in neat piles on the floor, on the backs of chairs. I made sure everything is tidy and perfect.

You're hopeless.

I get up, run my fingers through his silky leotards, scoop them up and bury my face in them and inhale. It smells of pollen and summer. I let them slide from my hands and walk back to the mirror.

You're pathetic.

My face stares at me, round and pale, with a pair of blue eyes. Overgrown uneven bangs.

What are you doing here? What hope do you have? You idiot. This isn't love, it's neediness and you know it. What are you to him? Nothing.

I pace the room.

No, there is something there. I sense something coming from him. Compassion.

I look in the mirror again.

Compassion? Compassion is not love. It comes from pity, from condolence, from remorse. You know what instills remorse? Dead people.

I sweep the bangs out of my face.

Then what is love, if not compassion?

A door slams a floor above.

I start, glance at the wall clock. It's after eight a.m.

My hands shake so badly, it takes me several tries to lock the door. I rush to the closet, get the broom, and dart to the performance hall. There is a faint echo of voices. I halt in the doorway.

Kostya and Pavlik stand on the stage, flustered. Sim sits in the first row. His arms are spread over the backs of the seats, his fingers sparkling with rings. A sequined scarf cradles his neck.

"Lis-ten!" he says.

They steal a glance at each other.

"What do you hear?" He leaps up.

Kostya tosses his hair back. "Sim, I'm not sure—"

"Be quiet!" His face turns red.

"But you asked—"

"I asked you to listen. Lis-ten."

I reach the end of the second row and stop.

Sweat glistens on Sim's forehead. He wipes it off with his scarf. "Put your hand on your heart. Like this. What do you hear? Music. Can you hear it? I'm asking you, can you hear it?"

They see me.

"What." Sim turns. "Ah, Irina. Perfect. Come here."

I circle the stage.

"Get down, both of you. I want you to sit and watch."

He lifts my face. I flinch, but his hands are warm and tender and not mean. "You don't need to talk to tell the audience your story. Words don't mean much. You need to let them hear your music."

I gulp.

"Sim, Irina—" begins Pavlik.

"I know. Don't interrupt me."

A heat wave flushes me.

"Don't be scared. You either have it or you don't. The stage will tell. Go on."

I stand frozen.

"I've seen you do it before. Go!" He claps.

My ears buzz and my knees feel weak.

They watch me. Kostya with a trace of distaste, Pavlik with curiosity. Sim waves me up. I mount the steps one by one and walk out to the middle of the stage, stopping by the orchestra pit, my legs and arms numb, my tongue stiff. My thoughts are garbled like strands of wool and I only know one thing: *I want to talk. I want to learn how to talk.*

"We're waiting."

"Sim," says Pavlik, "I'm sorry, but how can Irina perform if she doesn't know what you want her to do?"

Sim grimaces. "She knows. I know she does. Watch her."

He's so sure, so convinced of it, that I start believing. I put my hand on my heart and listen inside me, and hear it.

My music.

I'm still clutching the broom. I drop it on the floorboards. It clatters dully against the wood and it's the last sound I hear before another noise blots everything out. The grunts. Loud obnoxious grunts. There it sits, in the front row, a little to the right. The boar. I stick my hand in my pocket and find a sugar cube and take it out and beckon the boar to me. It snorts, rolls off the seat, and clops onstage. Saliva drips from its jaws. A pair of tusks gleam in the light. Two bloodshot piggy eyes swivel at me.

I hold out the sugar cube. *Come on, piggy, come and get it.*

It tips its head, roars, and charges straight at me.

I crouch with my legs wide apart, my fists raised.

When the boar is a couple of meters away from me, it springs. I punch it in the snout. It squeals and lands with a deafening thump. The force of the collision throws me off balance. I sit back, hard, but I don't cry out. The punch felt so good that in seconds I'm up and at the boar's side, kicking it and jabbing its hairy belly, striking it between its hind legs. It yelps, struggles to get to its feet. I can't stop. I want to pummel it to pulp. Sweat streams down my face and gets in my eyes.

Eat this, dickhead. Pervert. Asshole. Swine.

"More! More!" Sim springs up. "I want you to kill it! Kill it!"

I grin. It's like he opened a faucet. My pent up pain splashes and gurgles and rushes out. I stagger about the stage and bump into more beasts. They emerge from the shadows and set out at me, the catfish and the cockroach and two herrings.

Die, all of you. I strike left and right. *I want you to never bother me again. Perish. Cease to exist. Leave me alone!*

They melt into one pulsing blur. I grapple with something slippery, wrestle with something coarse. Smash, kick, hit with my fists and elbows and knees, slam them with my whole body. Then sharp pain rips up from my stomach. I bend and hold my knees, out of breath.

"Bravo! Brilliant! Brilliant!" Sim claps.

Pavlik joins him, then Kostya. The whole troupe is here, cheering me on, applauding.

Only one face is sour.

Shakalov stands in the door, his arms folded over his chest. He turns and leaves.

CHAPTER FIVE

HORSEFLIES

I'm afraid to close my eyes. I take out a slice of bread from under my jacket that's rolled up as a pillow and crumble it to small bits and eat it. My nerves are taut. The clock ticks off minutes after midnight. Darkness suffocates me but I don't want to switch on the light. Shakalov told me, "You're not an actress, you're a sweeper. Know your place, understand? You wait, I'll give you double-payment for this, dura." I've been listening for hours now. Nothing.

The empty theater is cold and quiet.

Is he coming?

Howling. There is howling in the corridor, a long drawn out wail. A patter of feet. I jump up, dizzy with fear. The hall beyond the door fills with the echo of yowls and snarls.

Damn you.

I grab the prop knife I found in one of the boxes. It's dull but it's something. The wailing is louder now as if the darkness itself is coming alive, thick with spite. I panic, drop the knife, stumble on the boxes and overturn them, and bump into the vanity table. Something tips and crashes to the floor with a bright clash. Glass shards spray in all directions. I touch the wall, feel around for the switch and can't find it.

The howling stops.

The jackal is sniffing at the door. I can hear its heavy breathing. I grope for my jacket and my backpack and that's when the keys jingle and the lock rasps and the door opens—

The mouse darts between the jackal's legs into a tunnel dug out of packed dirt. Roots trip it. Grit and grime blind its eyes. Behind it the jackal pants, gaining distance. The mouse squeaks, desperate. It knows that if it falters it will be dead. It scampers up, passes by the turtle's hollow, and bursts free into the street under the star-flecked sky.

The mouse can't pause, can't stop to catch its breath. Its tiny heart throbs with terror. It squirrels along the asphalt road close to the building walls and pelts into a narrow alley. Trash bins, acacia shrubs, parked cars in the labyrinth of inner courts and archways and yards. The mouse finds a crack in the wall behind a drainpipe, burrows inside and lies still.

I lean on a rough concrete wall of an apartment block, shivering from sitting for so long on the wet ground.

I should've seen it coming. Where will I go now?

In front of me is a square courtyard, desolate and damp

after the rain. An empty sandbox, a broken swing, and a couple of benches. Most windows in the building across the way are dark, a few aglow. One window on the first floor is open and through the lacy curtains wafts out the smell of fried onions. A hunched figure under a naked light bulb is cooking something in the middle of the night.

My stomach grumbles.

I stand up in the murky circle of streetlight. I'm somewhere deep in the bowels of old Moscow. A drunk couple wanders by, swaying and singing. I thumb up my backpack and steal after them in hopes of sneaking into the warmth of the entranceway. They stop by the heavy metal door, punch in the code, and disappear. I run up too late. It shuts with a resounding bang.

Bright lights splash over me. A car rolls along the sidewalk and vanishes behind a utility shack at the end of the yard.

Maybe I can catch the driver entering.

I follow, skirt a cluster or chokeberry bushes, and come upon a dead end. It's milling with figures and glowing streaks of smoldering cigarettes and hushed talking.

I hide behind the bushes and watch through the gaps.

Car lights flash, tear out silhouettes from the night. About ten girls in heels and minis and cheap fur jackets smoke and step from foot to foot like tousled chickens. A stocky man climbs out of the car and saunters up to them. He talks to one, and not a minute later, they drive off. Another car rolls up. I'm rooted to the ground.

This is my future. Pick-a-hooker drive-though. Better this, better someone nameless. In, out, done. Never to see again.

I pick a chokeberry. It's juicy and astringent.

A militia model 6 Lada parks and a couple militants file out on unsteady legs, their caps askew. They fetch a pair of giggling girls. I gape after them until the red taillights wink out in the darkness.

Fucking slime bags.

I want to leave but the forbidden and the dirty holds me with an unhealthy attraction.

The last girl is gone. I have eaten so many berries that my stomach aches and I shiver from cold and exhaustion. I decide to stay awake and wait for the early risers to begin leaving the building for work so that I can slip inside one of the entranceways and curl up and nap on the warm top landing.

A hand falls on my shoulder.

My heart plummets. I wheel around and see five guys in their twenties, dark beanies pulled down to their brows. Smug faces, brutish eyes, beer and smoke breath, and randy sneers.

"Hey, beautiful. Looking for a job?"

My blood stills.

Hostile buzzing sniggers.

Horseflies.

I back up and I smash into the bramble.

They draw closer, interested and excited. Size me up.

"Why are you so quiet?"

I should've taken the prop knife.

A hand flicks on a lighter and holds it to my face. "Did you hear what Uncle Roma said? Answer, slut."

"Maybe she's, you know..."

"Why don't you ask her."

"Hey, beautiful, are you retarded?"

"She's scared. Don't be scared, you can talk to Uncle Roma. I'll be gentle. I won't touch a single hair on your pretty head, only on your pussy."

They crack up, thrilled and nervous.

My stomach fills with lead.

"Talk, I said!" Roma's eyes grow into compound spheres. Clear wings unfold from his back. "Say, 'Hello, Uncle Roma. I want to suck your dick.'" He grabs my chin.

I kick him in the groin.

He throttles me. I gasp for breath—

The horseflies chase the mouse out of the bushes and into a dank entrance with the broken code lock. Here they push it in the corner and fall on it and sting it one by one. Their hairy abdomens expand and gorge with blood and shake from excitement and aggression. The mouse twitches on the floor. They cover it, rise when it moves, settle and suck on its belly and by the tail between its hind legs and everywhere they can find exposed, vulnerable flesh.

A dog barks behind a door.

Slow and sluggish, the horseflies lift and hang over the mouse. It's swollen from bites.

The dog senses them and barks and barks and doesn't stop.

Spooked, the horseflies surge into the shadows and vanish.

I unglue my eyelids. I'm swaying lightly, lying on a hard bench, surrounded by the smell of disinfectant and the whoop of a siren. I'm in an ambulance. Everything below my waist is screaming.

A woman's face lowers over mine.

"Shhh. You're fine. We're ten minutes away."

Lulled by the movement, I pass out.

Arms heave me up and roll me off the cot onto a gurney, and

wheel me between glass doors under bluish fluorescent lights.

Flat, tired voices call out.

"Natasha, where do you want her?"

"What's she got?"

"Vaginal bleeding."

"Eighth floor. The rest are full."

Vaginal bleeding. Great. I hope your brat is gone, Lyosha Kabansky.

I'm trundled into a freight elevator. The cabin jitters upward, stops. The doors roll open.

"Galina Viktorovna! Girls!"

"What?"

"I've got a bleeding one. Where do you want her?"

Lights blind me. I squint and make out a nurse relaying something to a sleepy woman in a crumpled lab coat who looks like a mole. She screws her myopic eyes and waves off the nurse and pushes me into a shabby examination room.

Greenish walls, a brown vinyl bench, a battered gynecological chair, and a desk with a clunky computer. She sits on a chair next to me and jots something down in a journal.

I study her. No neck, weak eyes and ears, graying hair pulled into a bun, powerful arms. She sniffs the air. "Myshko, Irina Anatolievna?"

I nod.

"What happened?"

I don't move.

"Can you hear me?"

Do you care?

"Answer, please. I haven't got all night."

I lift my arms then decide against it.

"Are you a deaf-mute?" She raises non-existent brows.

I gaze back, defiant.

"So, Irina. Either you answer me or I will have to call militia and have them talk to you." She reaches for my backpack at the foot of the gurney.

I intercept her hand, mime writing.

"That's better." She gives me a blank prescription sheet and a pen and watches me write.

Red splotches crawl up her cheeks. "Attacked by horseflies? What's this nonsense?"

It's not nonsense, it's the truth.

She stands up without a word, washes her big red hands in the tiny sink and dries them on a grubby towel before slapping on gloves.

"Lie still."

She lifts my shirt and feels my stomach.

I bite my lip to stifle a cry.

Her fingers enter me.

"Last period?"

I shrug.

She pokes her head in the door and yells. "Laskin! Quick!"

A young balding man shows up. A scrawny weasel. "You asked for me, Galina Viktorovna?" His eyes fix below my waist.

I yank up my panties.

"I need an ultrasound."

"One minute." He turns on the computer, pulls the gurney closer, squirts cool jelly on my stomach, and smears it with the probe. The screen is blue, then black, then there are rows of numbers and a shimmering slice of a circle, a grainy image composed of white lines.

Laskin moves the probe around, presses in and holds it in one spot. A black oval hole appears, and inside it is a grainy blob with a head, a body, and two bumps. They move.

"About two months?" says Laskin.

And it suddenly hits me.
It's my baby, it's alive. It's waving at me.
It doesn't know that I want to kill it.

CHAPTER SIX

EAGLET

It's morning. Sun streams through the window at the end of the hallway, weak and cheerless. Shadows dance on the greenish hospital walls and curtains move on the breeze from the cracked pane. It doesn't help. The air stinks of antiseptic and wet floor rags and unwashed women's bodies. The wall space between doors is occupied by portable beds. On each sits a girl my age or younger wrapped in a plush robe and accompanied by a worried mother.

A flock of sheep poised for slaughter.

I sit on a bed at the far end, alone, waiting for my turn for an abortion. I rub my eyes. I'm tired but I can't sleep.

The door by the window opens. A stocky surgeon pulls down his mask. "Ovechkina!"

The plump ruddy girl sitting on the bed across from mine answers. "Me."

"Come in." He withdraws.

Her cotton-socked feet search for slippers. She must be not much older than fifteen, no mother at her side, only a crinkly plastic bag of mandarins. She throws me a suspicious glance and shoves them under the pillow and staggers off.

I smell oatmeal, black bread, and cafeteria tea.

"Breakfast!"

A piggy lady in a greasy apron and a cook's hat appears from behind the corner. She pushes a steel cart loaded with steaming pots, and stops next to me. "You for an abortion?"

I stare at the food, hungry.

"Yes? No? You can't eat before an abortion, didn't the doctor tell you? You must go on an empty stomach."

I hesitate.

"Well?"

I shake my head no and greedily watch her ladle porridge onto a chipped plate and stick in a bent aluminum spoon. She adds a slice of bread, pours tea in a glass, and hands them both to me.

"Breakfast!"

Doors creak open. Sleepy women in housecoats shuffle out and receive their ration. I slurp hot tea, put the glass on the floor, place the plate on my bended knees, and dig in. The oatmeal is watery and salty and in every spoonful I find at least one oat husk. I don't care. Within minutes it's gone. I lick the spoon, then the plate, clean. I'm still hungry. I eat the bread and finish the tea, then shamble across the corridor and plunge my hand under the pillow and pull a couple of mandarins from the bag. I shove them in my mouth together with the skin.

My cheeks grow hot.

I hope I'll wait long enough to catch lunch.

A nurse trots up, pulls Ovechkina's empty bed into the surgery room, and a few minutes later, rolls it out with the girl covered to her chin with a thin cotton sheet and an IV attached to her dangling arm. She parks the bed in its place and my heart stills. The girl's lips are so white they're blue, her eyelids are paper-thin and there is no color in her face.

You killed your baby because you didn't want it, like me. Maybe it's mercy to kill the one whom you know you won't be able to love. My mama didn't want me. I wonder why she kept me. She should've disposed of me like I will dispose of Lyosha's brat.

I hit my stomach. I want the thing inside of me to feel it.

"Myshko!"

I start.

"Myshko!" The surgeon passes his eyes from girl to girl. They all look at their mothers and at each other.

The same nurse marches up to me. "Myshko, Irina?"

I nod, suddenly numb.

"Did you eat anything today?" She has a thin neck, like a goose, and large stupid eyes.

I don't know why but I point to my crotch.

"Do you need to go to the restroom? Well, what have you been waiting for, sitting here all this time? Go. Quick."

I walk to the door where I've seen women come and go, close it behind me, and lower the hook in the rusty eyelet and hold on to the sink, a sour taste in my mouth and my gut twisted.

What happened? What are you afraid of?

The toilet stinks of piss. A forty-watt bulb hangs by a cord from the ceiling. Cracked ceramic tile walls, cloudy mirror above the sink, and a yellowing shower pan behind a cheap plastic curtain printed with hideous flowers.

I don't think long.

It's been over a month. They'll wait.

I pee, strip, turn on the water, and step into the scalding stream. It burns my skin. Steam rises in billows and fogs up the mirror. Somebody forgot a lump of soap. I pick it up, lather my hair and scratch my scalp until it stops itching, and scrub my skin with my hands and nails. It stings between my thighs. I bite my lip and carefully peel apart every fold and wash myself clean. My skin turns red. I stand under the water letting it roll over me.

The door rattles.

"Who's there?" A woman's voice. "How much longer?"

I open my eyes and slam into the wall.

Lyosha's face looks at me from the shower curtain.

You can't be here, get out.

It changes into Roma's, then into one of his mates, and into Shakalov's. It shifts and grimaces and elongates and slides off the perspiring plastic and curdles into fat, milky maggots. Their squirming bodies drop to my feet. I shriek and stomp on them and squish them. Gobs more squirt out of every crack between the tiles and boil out of the toilet bowl and flop over the edge of the sink and drop to the floor with wet smacks.

I hate you.

I trample them, shaking from revulsion. They pop with awful squelching noises and more of them slither out of every hole, pulsing and shiny.

Leave me alone. Leave me alone!

I press into the corner, my wet hair sticking to my face.

The maggots cover the floor, clump together, and coagulate into a shape that darkens and grows fur and legs and a snout.

The boar.

It grunts and clops its hooves on the edge of the pan and labors over.

You think I can't hurt you? I can. I will murder your brat.

The boar stops and tilts its head as if it listens.

They'll scrape it out of me and chop it up and flush it down the toilet for Moscow sewage rats to eat. It doesn't deserve to live. It's ugly like you, Lyosha Kabansky.

There are voices by the door. It rattles. The rusty hook gives. I lift my leg to kick the boar and my other foot slides and I fall and hit the back of my head on the pan.

I come to with a throbbing headache. A rough hospital blanket tickles my chin. A face blocks the light. It's Galina Viktorovna and she is furious.

"Were you trying to kill yourself, or what?"

Pain stabs at my temples. I wince.

"Shower! Who told you that you could take a shower?"

Please, don't talk.

"You could've broken your neck." She sniffs the air. "You could've had a miscarriage. And then what? What if not all of it came out? We'd have to scrape you clean and that could sterilize you. At sixteen years old! What if you wanted to get pregnant again?"

I don't want any babies. Not now, not ever. Cut out my whole uterus if you want.

No, says a small screeching voice.

I sit up, bewildered.

The voice is coming from my stomach. I peer down at it, feel it with my hand.

Butchering me won't hurt Lyosha. He doesn't care for me. He doesn't even know about my existence.

Who are you?

I'm an eaglet.

But, my head spins, *I thought you were a piglet.*
No, I'm not. Although I'd eat one. Or a couple. Or a boar.
So you will grow into—
An eagle. If you let me.
If I let you.
And if you feed me. Boars, jackals, I'm not picky.
Any of them?
Any of them. Please.

"Are you listening? You missed your spot!"

I look at Galina Viktorovna and shake my head.

"What's that supposed to mean?"

I go through the pantomime.

"You're not going to do an abortion?" Her face turns spiteful. "Well, suit yourself. But you can't stay here. We're not a hotel, you know. Gather your stuff. I'll sign you out." She leaves.

I change in the restroom and look for the reception desk. Walking hurts. Every part of my groin is raw and chafing. I can't ride the metro like this. I take out my notebook and pen and write a note.

"Please call The Chamber Theater and ask for Pavel Baboch. Tell him to come and pick me up. Thank you. Irina Myshko."

I hand the paper to the toad behind the counter. Her mouth is so wide that when she opens it I think her head will split in two.

"Theater? You want me to call a theater?"

I nod.

She smirks and dials.

I wait, gazing at the patients and their visitors sitting on the benches along the wall. Talking, moaning, complaining.

"Hello? Chamber Theater? This is First Clinical Hospital

calling. I have a patient here, Myshko, Irina Anatolievna."

I don't breathe. It's Monday. He should be there.

"I told you, First Clinical!" She taps the pen on the counter. "What? Ma'am, how would I know? I see her for the first time in my life."

Please, Ilinichna. Please.

"She's asking for Pavel Baboch. Yes." The toad woman fires off the clinic address and slams down the receiver. "Wait over there." She goes back to her crossword puzzle.

My heart explodes.

He's coming, he's really coming.

I drop onto the empty bench in the corner and study the walls for something to do to calm down. A large round clock, a dead plant in a macramé pot, a bulletin board.

VACUUM ABORTION OF A NINE-WEEK OLD CHILD.

I fixate on it. My palms turn clammy. It's a thick paperboard with four graphic illustrations glued to it. In one, a sharp metal tool enters a uterus; in the next one, a fetus is sucked out; next, it's crushed; and in the last, its bloody body parts and a torn-off head are scooped into the trash.

I shudder. *Eaglet?*

Silence.

Is it okay if I call you eaglet? I put a hand on my stomach.

Yes. Same voice. *You can call me eaglet.*

I'm sorry I wanted to kill you.

It's okay.

I'm glad I didn't.

Me too.

I can't think of anything else.

Two hours pass. Every time the doors slams, I flinch. Shoes clack on the floor. The elevator whines up and down. People trickle past me. Visitors with flowers, boxes of candy, and oilcloth bags stuffed with food. I turn numb and only notice Pavlik when he squats in front of me.

"Irina! What are you doing here? What happened?"

I'm afraid he'll hear my heartbeat.

He is dressed in a fine wool coat and a cashmere scarf, impeccable, a fresh scent of the street on him. I watch his lips part and his eyes dance with worry, and I want to touch his hair and stick my face in it and sniff it.

"Ilinichna told me you asked me to pick you up."

I want to say how happy I am that he came. The words gets stuck at my teeth and I feel crippled by this debilitating muteness like never before, and I drop my face in my hands.

"Can you walk?" This touch, this look he gives me.

Can it be?

I take his hand and—

The mouse is weightless. It floats after the butterfly, mesmerized by the black velvet scales of its wings. It sniffs. The butterfly smells of pollen, warm wind, and summer. It flutters, somewhat erratic, out of the hospital building and into the street parking lot, mostly empty save for a couple of dusty Volgas, an ambulance van, and a shiny new Mercedes.

A blue macaw is perched on the rim of the driver's door, its head inclined and its eyes impatient.

Kostya.

CHAPTER SEVEN

MACAW

I climb into Kostya's car, into the expensive smells of new leather, cigarette smoke, and cologne. Tinted windows. Grebenshchikov sings from the speakers about a golden city, a lion, an ox, and an eagle. I stroke the smooth seat. Pavlik sits next to me. Our knees touch and I freeze. He doesn't notice. Kostya takes one last drag, flicks out the stub, pops a piece of gum into his mouth, and starts the engine.

The car rolls forward.

"Where to?" says Pavlik.

I look in his eyes. Too dark. If I stare any longer I'll fall in and drown.

Kostya salutes to the balding guard at the gate. He regards us with indifference. We drive onto the street and merge with traffic to honks from a large blue truck with BREAD stenciled on its side in large white letters.

"Oh, shut up. Learn how to drive, peasant." Kostya pops a bubble.

"Irina, where do you want us to drop you off?" says Pavlik.

I take out my notepad and write. "I don't know."

"You don't know?"

Kostya throws an irritated glance in the rearview mirror.

We stop at the light.

I sit up straight. There is a noise on the periphery of my hearing, an echo of a blast. Maybe an engine misfired. Grebenshchikov sings about a girl watching lions out of her window. I look out of the window and I see no lions, only dull apartment blocks and hunched figures crawling along the street like bugs in pursuit of survival. Typical Moscow, yet something about it is wrong. The way the air stands still and the way it's quiet. I have a growing feeling of unease.

"How about we go to my place?" says Pavlik. "We'll have some tea and you'll have time to decide."

"Great idea," says Kostya, and revs up the engine.

We jolt, weave in and out of traffic gaps, cut off other drivers. Kostya's face is calm, his left pinky on the wheel and his right hand casually speed-shifting.

My stomach jumps to my throat and sits there, throbbing.

"Kostya, please. I'd appreciate it if you delivered us in one piece."

"You're insulting me." He blows out a bubble and smacks it and sucks it in. His jaws are working with fury and determination.

"Do I sense hostility?"

"Calm down, everything is fine. If you'll excuse me, I'd like to concentrate on driving."

I perk up. The unease is stronger.

"This is just great." Kostya slams the brakes.

We lurch off the seats.

The broad five-lane avenue is congested. It's stop-and-go.

"Strange," says Pavlik. "I don't remember it ever being so bad."

Kostya winds down the window and lights a cigarette.

City noises drift in, a distant whine of militia.

"Probably another rally," says Pavlik. "Pensioners worshipping Stalin so he'll rise from the grave and end their misery by sending them to Gulag. Free lodging, free food, free expedited death."

I look at Pavlik. *Will you believe me if I tell you I saw Lenin break woodpeckers' necks?*

"Gulag? No, thanks. I'd rather die onstage," says Kostya.

"Agreed."

"How terribly unoriginal."

They crack up.

I stop listening. A movement catches my eye. A bird lands on the roof of an apartment building. I crane up my neck to see. It's large and black and has a bald red head.

A vulture.

"I'm going around." Kostya shifts in reverse, swerves into the opposite lane, skirts a bus, and nears a red light when a loud blast shakes the air and the ground.

Several car alarms go off. A flock of pigeons scatters.

"Wow!" Kostya slams on the breaks.

"What was that?" Pavlik's voice trembles.

The car stands right on the crosswalk. An old hag in a tattered coat trundles across the street, and when she's level with the Mercedes, she lifts her cane and slams it onto the hood.

"Hey!" Kostya chokes on his gum. "What the hell are you

doing?"

She shakes the cane at him and sputters curses with blunt stubbornness.

Goat, you are a goat.

"Did you see that? She hit my car!" Kostya pulls on the parking break, gets out, and towers over the old woman, yelling and waving his arms.

Pavlik sighs. "I'll be right back."

I stay put.

Another blast rocks the street.

Pavlik ducks. Drivers step out and shout to each other.

My flesh prickles in goose bumps. I hear a new noise, a series of piercing avian screams. They rise and fall and loop in the sky overhead.

Vultures getting ready to feast on roadkill.

I watch the woman, horrified.

She turns her head and fixes a pair of wet, translucent eyes on me as if she can see me sitting in the back of the car. Her face sprouts matted fur. Her large nose flattens, her skin shrivels and gives way to a mangy hide from which greasy wool begins falling out in clumps. Her limbs unhinge and fold backward, and where she stood a moment ago sits a sick, dying goat. A pair of vultures circle above it, casting their bald reddish heads from side to side.

The carcass strippers waiting for the goat to die.

One bird lifts its head and snaps at me.

I recoil.

Kostya and Pavlik get back in the car, silent and fuming.

We turn into Novyy Arbat. There are fewer pedestrians here and hardly any cars. The blasts come at regular intervals of every few minutes and send a rattling report along the street.

"Look." Kostya points. "The White House is on fire."

"Oh God," says Pavlik. "Oh God."

We're one block away from the Freedom Square. On both sides of the street people are running. I wipe the glass with my sleeve to see better. Two top floors of the White House are visible over the roofs. Billows of black smoke burst from the windows high into the sky.

Kostya gives gas and the car lurches forth.

"It must be connected to Ostankino's storming yesterday. Kostya, we need to get out of here." Pavlik is pale.

Ostankino was stormed? I smirk. *I can see how that went. A bunch of donkeys with dicks for brains who don't know shit about politics took to the streets. Hey, storming a television center is more exciting than watching TV and chugging bootleg. No hope of getting laid, no money for a whore, let me gun a couple of douche bags to give my hands something to do because I'm tired of wanking.*

"Are you joking?" says Kostya. "Where is your patriotism? Your love for motherland? The history of Russia is unfolding in front of your very eyes." He is trying to laugh but it comes out strained.

"And you're so eager to become a part of this history?"

"Let's watch them blow each other up, the dumb peasants."

"Kostya, please." Pavlik pulls on his arm.

"You know what, you bore me to tears sometimes. You can walk from here if you want, I'm staying to see what happens."

Pavlik stares. "Have you lost your mind?"

We stop at the square.

Civilians crowd the sidewalk. A handful of tanks squat on the plaza in front of the White House. There are cries and bursts of gunfire. Men with Kalashnikov rifles crouch behind the streetlights, sit on top of the tanks, aim and fire. It smells of smoke. The road ahead is blocked by a barricade of crates and overturned park benches and other junk. A couple of burned out buses lie on their sides, smoldering. People mill between fires by the barricade as if it's a picnic.

A tank rotates its turret and fires. The explosion is so loud it reverberates in my chest.

"Kostya, get us out of here!"

"Shit, this is exciting." Kostya winds down the passenger window and shouts at a group of onlookers. "Guys, any idea about what is going on?"

"Listen to me." Pavlik shakes his shoulder.

"Coup d'etat!" says a bearded man with a camera.

Next I hear a strange whistle. The man with the camera drops to the ground. A dark spot soaks the back of his shirt and rapidly grows bigger.

People shriek.

"Snipers!"

"Snipers on the roofs!"

Vultures. My feet get cold.

The crowd breaks up, leaving the man to die.

"He got shot. He got shot." Kostya just looks.

"Fucking go!"

Pavlik's hysterical cry jolts Kostya out of his stupor and he gives gas and the car lunges forward. We drive through screams and gunfire and ambulance whine and black acrid smoke. The Mercedes skids on the corner and careens to the right. I slam into the door and wince. We fly along one narrow alleyway after another and finally veer into a parking lot stacked with a handful of prefabricated metal garages and a few cars, and grind to a stop.

Kostya storms out.

"I'm sorry, Irina." Pavlik follows him.

I watch them fight under a yellowing elm.

Kostya shouts. Pavlik grabs him by the shoulders and

shakes him.

Then I hear it. An avian screech coming from the roof. And I know what's about to happen.

Isn't that what you wanted, Irina Myshko?

Guilt and shame flush my face. I hope I have enough time. I jump out and squint, putting a hand over my eyes to locate the source of the noise.

You fucking piece of birdshit.

On the roof of the five-story Khrushchovka sits a vulture. It cocks and aims and I leap for the elm.

The sky crackles.

A few yellowing leaves break off and seesaw in the air. Kostya sways and topples headlong to the ground. I slam into Pavlik. We fall down hard and roll to a stop by the wheels of a ratty Zaporozhets. Three more shots fire in rapid succession. I scramble to my knees and hands and hook Pavlik by the armpits and drag him further behind the car out of the sniper's field of vision. Bullets hit the asphalt not two steps away from where we were seconds ago. Hairs stand up on my neck. Sweat trickles down my back and my heart hammers so loudly I think I will faint.

"I'm shot...I'm shot..." Pavlik cradles his thigh in one hand, blood seeping through his fingers. He looks at me with wide, frightened eyes. "Kostya...where is Kostya?" he asks, and passes out.

For a moment or two I can't breathe, then I scream a horrible animal cry. I scream and scream and scream until my throat is scratchy and I can't scream anymore. Wind tousles my hair. It smells like it's about to rain. I drop my head and hold my face in my hands—

The mouse sits by the butterfly. Its black wings are torn and its abdomen is cut; thick dark liquid drips from it and pools into a puddle. The butterfly doesn't move. The mouse squeaks at it, nudges it with its nose. A bird lies next to the butterfly, a macaw, a long-tailed indigo parrot. Its plumage is so bright and blue, it puts the sky to shame. The macaw doesn't move, it's very still. There is a horrid gash in its chest.

It's dead.

CHAPTER EIGHT

WALRUS

I don't remember how or when the ambulance picked us up. All I remember is hands. Insistent hands that tried to pry me away from Pavlik. They stopped after a while. I wouldn't let go. Not when they washed him or drugged him or cut the bullet from his leg. I'm with him day and night. I eat what other patients give me and I stand over his bed and watch his face, waiting for him to wake up. In five days he hasn't opened his eyes once.

"You can't stay here," says the mustached doctor with big meaty hands. He is a tired and irritated walrus.

I squeeze the metal bar of Pavlik's bed. It's at the very end of a long, overflowing room—thirty patients where there should be only twenty. Beds are crammed in crooked rows, helter-skelter, some are separated by curtain partitions, some are not.

Tiled walls in need of a good scrubbing. Piss pots, IV stands. Cold artificial light.

I'm not going anywhere. You'll have to make me.

"She sleeps in the closet by the canteen," says a man's voice from behind the partition on the left.

"What do you mean, sleeps," says the doctor.

I study the floor.

After a couple of wet, repulsive coughs, the voice behind the partition continues. "I saw her sneak out this morning. I was leaving from breakfast and there she goes, quiet as a mouse, slipping through the door. And I thought, I said to myself, I have to tell the doctor."

"What is wrong with you? What a bitter man. Let the girl be," says a wrinkly patient from the bed across from us. Most of his head is wrapped in gauze. He props himself up on his elbows. "Don't listen to him, Igor Martynovich. She's no trouble. She loves the boy. Stands over him from morning till night, just stands there and looks and looks." He grins a toothless smile. "Let the girl stay."

My face grows hot. I want to vanish.

Curious heads lift from adjacent beds. And voices.

"Yes, let her stay."

"She's cute."

"Something to look at in this rathole."

"You want me to allow a girl to sleep in a men's ward?" The doctor rounds on them. "Anything else? Should I maybe give her a bed too, for you to visit? I haven't slept in my own bed since Monday, too busy nannying you. Something to look at." He snorts and turns to me. "You need to go." But there is no madness in his voice, only exhaustion.

I'm staying.

"Look." He is so close I can smell coffee and cheap

cigarettes on his breath. "Go home and don't worry. He is young, he'll recover in no time. Compared to the rest of what I have here, it's nothing. Pierced artery, big deal. The bullet didn't even touch his bone. He'll be walking in a few weeks. But I can't let you stay here. It's not a hotel, it's a hospital, do you understand?"

I shake my head from side to side. *He's the closest I ever got to home. I have no other home to go to.*

"No? Well, you leave me no choice. When I'm back for the evening checkup, I want you gone. Otherwise, I'll have to call militia." He leaves.

I stare after him for what feels like hours.

"Irina?"

At first I think I imagined it.

Pavlik struggles to sit up. He is weak and pale, almost translucent.

I drop to my knees at his bed, one big stupid smile. *You're awake! I've been waiting for this. I've been waiting and waiting and waiting.* The words die on the tip of my tongue. I bite it until it bleeds.

"Where am I?" His eyes sweep the room. Wonder changes to dread. "What happened? Where is Kostya?"

Kostya is dead and I'm glad I'm mute.

"Please, tell me. I can see that you know."

I picture Kostya, how he fell, how his golden hair fanned out on the asphalt, how I thought about wanting to see him shot for calling me a peasant and guilt eats me alive. Guilt and hurt and rage. I want to find every vulture and kill it.

"Please."

I'm afraid he'll cry. I rummage in my backpack for the

notepad and take a long time, as if I can't find it.

"My leg." He moans, lifts the blanket, studies the bandage, then carefully touches it.

"A sniper got you," says the voice from behind the partition.

"A sniper? Oh God." Pavlik's hand shakes. "Oh God." He probes around with a finger and winces. "How long have I been here?"

"Since Monday." A long wet cough. "Them surgeons took—"

"What's today?"

"Saturday."

"Saturday?"

I pretend I can't find the pen.

"What, a whole week has gone?"

I nod.

"I can't believe it." He holds his face. "All I remember is that man, that big man with a camera. Kostya was asking him something. Then he fell. People started screaming, 'snipers, snipers on the roof.' After that, nothing."

"This girl saved your life," says the wrinkly man. "Igor Martynovich told me. She wrapped her shirt around your leg, like a tourniquet. That's what stopped the blood flow."

Pavlik looks at me.

I stare at my feet, at my dirty sneakers with threadbare laces tied into knots. *Enough, Irina Myshko. Stop it. The more you hope, the worse it'll be. Saving his life won't make him suddenly love you. Get it through your thick skull.*

"Is that true?"

I don't move.

"Irina."

I'm paralyzed.

Pavlik lapses into a pensive silence.

We stay like this for a long time.

Footsteps jerk me out of slumber.

A middle-aged couple stops by the foot of Pavlik's bed. They both wear glasses. The woman is tall and slick and neatly dressed, her dark locks are cut into a wavy bob. She has green eyes and her protruding ears are adorned with dangling malachite earrings. The man is shorter and squatter. Wool suit. Graying hair. Vacant stare.

"Mama! Papa!" Pavlik sits up.

"Pavlusha." The woman glides to him, props him up on the pillow, and sits on the edge of the bed. There is something poisonous in the way she moves and she doesn't blink. The man hobbles after her. He turns his entire head to look over me and his face lights up with strange delight.

I wonder if mama ever thinks about where I am. What happened to me, am I alive or dead. Does she care?

"There you are." The woman's voice is controlled. A tear glistens on her cheek. She quickly wipes it off.

"Mama..." says Pavlik.

They formally peck each other on the cheeks.

"Pavlusha, our dear Pavlusha," says the man. "We called every hospital. We started to think that maybe—"

"Anton." She gives him a glare as if she wants to fry him.

"Forgive me, Yulechka." His lips press into a thin line. It makes his eyes look bigger and rounder.

"Maybe what?" says Pavlik.

"Nothing," says Anton. "Nothing. How are you feeling?"

"I'm okay."

They lift the blanket and examine the bandaged wound and

talk. It's all very banal and empty. Facts about things. About the political crisis and the shootout by the White House, and the number of victims, and the mysterious snipers whom nobody can identify, and the consequences of bullet wounds and recovery times. Pavlik keeps asking about Kostya, and they keep dodging his questions.

"Did he call?"

They shrug and shake heads.

"Did his father call?"

Another shrug.

They know. I can feel it. The way they avert their eyes and avoid direct answers.

"Irina," says Pavlik.

I tense.

Anton drills me with a questioning glance.

"Please. Just tell me. Is Kostya—"

"What is it with you. Kostya, Kostya. Let's talk about you," says Yulia.

"I'm okay, Mama. I promise." He puts on a stage smile.

"That's the spirit." Anton pats him on the shoulder.

"Are you sure you're okay?" She licks her lips.

I stare at her forked tongue. *A viper. A venomous viper.*

"I'm sure."

"Then why didn't you call us?"

Nice bite.

"Mama, I just woke up!"

"Well, somebody should've called us." She measures me with her green eyes as if it's my fault. "We were beyond ourselves with grief, we thought you might've died." She covers her face.

"Yulechka!" Anton makes a hooting noise.

And I know what he is. *An owl.*

"Be quiet. Can't you see he's distressed?"

"Irina." The corners of Pavlik's lips turn up a little. "I'm sorry I haven't introduced you. My loving parents, Yulia Davydovna and Anton Borisovich."

I hold back a grin.

"Mama, Papa, this is Irina Myshko, my colleague from the theater. A very talented actress, Sim's newest find."

They look at me as if I'm dinner. I endure the uncomfortable silence. *Don't be rude, say something. At least cuss me out. Anything but this cultured abhorrence.*

They wait for me to talk.

"Oh, I'm sorry, I forgot to mention. Irina is mute."

"A mute actress?" Anton is bemused. "How does that work, I don't quite understand. Do you mime? Are you deaf-mute? Is she deaf-mute?" he asks Pavlik.

"No, Papa. She can hear very well."

"That's strange. Why doesn't she talk, do you know? There must be a reason, there's always a reason. Maybe she has a birth defect of some sort?"

Pavlik's face hardens.

I said the wrong word at the wrong time to the wrong woman.

There is a ringing silence in the ward. The patients are eavesdropping on the conversation to mull over it later.

"By the way," says Pavlik, "if not for Irina, I'd be in a morgue right now instead of a clinic."

"Pavlusha!" Yulia's nostrils flare. "You mustn't say it. Don't say things like that. It's bad luck."

"Mama, please. Don't."

"Did you really?" says Anton.

"She did," comes from the bed across from Pavlik. "The doctor himself told me."

They all look at me. Yulia, Anton, the patients, the janitor with a mop, the passing nurse. I shrink, suddenly aware of my matted hair, uncombed for days, my crumpled clothes and scuffed sneakers and unwashed smell.

"Baboch, Anton Borisovich. Please accept my gratitude." He smiles and shakes my unresisting hand.

"Yulia Davydovna. I'm touched by your interest for my son's life. If it is indeed true, I thank you." Yulia offers me her hand as if she expects me to kiss it.

"You never mentioned any Irina to me," she tells Pavlik. "How long have you been working together?"

"About a month."

"You mean to say, of all the girls in the theater you picked the one who's mute?"

"Mama, I told you. We're colleagues. There is nothing between us."

My heart stops. *There is nothing between us. There is nothing between us.*

Pavlik talks about being just friends and communicating without words and my talent and my audition. Yulia talks about how it always begins with being just friends. Anton talks about a mute actress being a potentially profitable sensation and what a smart move it is on Sim's part.

I try to listen and I can't. My ears won't work. My eyes sting. I flicker and—

The viper hisses, uncoils in a predatory dance. The mouse scurries off but the owl blocks its way. A heavy thud makes them jump. The giant walrus has arrived. It brays, its tusks gleaming with menace. The owl hoots in response, props the butterfly up on its wing. The viper slithers next to it. They vanish down the corridor.

The mouse dashes after them but its short legs can't carry it fast enough. Soon they're out of sight and the mouse is lost in the maze of endless hallways. Confused and frightened, it panics, runs around in circles, then stops and sniffs the air. The smell of rain comes on a draft from behind a corner. The mouse follows its nose and soon it's in the vestibule and out the front doors.

City noises stun it. The sky is shrouded with clouds. It's pouring rain. The air is dank and cold and everything is dripping. The owl with the butterfly and the viper get inside a new model 9 Lada, the color of wheat, and drive off.

The mouse watches them, drenched to the bone.

I stand on the steps of the hospital's colonnaded porch and look at the avenue heavy with traffic. Cars splash through puddles. Pedestrians bustle back and forth under umbrellas like wet glistening bugs. Water drips down my face and seeps under my shirt. I clasp my elbows to stop from shivering.

Did you expect to be invited like some honorary hero? Take a good look at yourself. You're fat, mute, and ugly, without a kopeck in your pocket. No one needs you, Irina Myshko.

I descend onto the street and walk in the downpour.

I don't care. I will find him.

CHAPTER NINE

BOAR

I kick open the door to the Tsvetnoy Boulevard station. Warm air bastes my face like the breath of an underground beast. I sneeze, shake the water off my hair, unzip my jacket, wring it out, and stuff it in my backpack. I merge with the throng of bodies and skip through the turnstile. I'm on the escalator long before the booth attendant shouts, "Hooligan! Get back! Pay the fare!" I hold on to the conveyor belt, ride down the inclined shaft, walk under a marble arch, and join commuters on the narrow platform.

The clock above the tunnel says it's 12:54 p.m.

I'm hungry, wet, and cold, and I try not to breathe. It smells of earth, wet newspaper, cabbage soup, and sweat. The staccato of the train echoes somewhere deep in the tube. It will be here any moment, the tapeworm.

The rhythm of the rails picks up in volume. People cram the edge of the platform. I move with them and sense someone behind me, and I know it's him. The heaviness of the steps, the breathing pattern, the snorting. The hairs on my back stand up. His stare strips me bare. He's singling me out for a quickie.

Hello, boar. Long time no see.

Boar? says the eaglet. *Can I have it? I'm hungry.*

Eaglet! My feet get cold. *I forgot about you. I'm sorry. So many things have happened.*

It's okay. I forgot about myself too and *now I woke up and remembered. Will you feed me?*

Yes. Yes, I will.

The train arrives. Before the doors open completely, before the exiting passengers can clamber out, the mob pushes in and elbows its way through. I let myself be carried with them, grab on to the greasy bar, and hang over the heads of those who managed to get seated.

"Be careful, the doors are closing," says a bland recorded voice. "The next stop is Chekhovskaya. Dear passengers, please make way for the elderly and the invalids."

Too bad "invalid" isn't written on my face.

The doors slam shut and the train lurches.

A heavy palm lands on my ass and squeezes it.

You stinky bastard, you perverted piece of shit.

Are these names for a boar? says the eaglet.

Not for any boar, only for this one.

I twist around.

At first I can only stare. Despite my efforts, a gasp escapes me. Lyosha gawps at me, unblinking and unbelieving. Then he begins to laugh. He wears the same grimy sweater ragged to threads on his paunch, and a pair of training pants, his favorite.

Easy to slip off and to pull out his dick. His piggy eyes narrow. He seizes my wrist.

"I'll be damned. Irkadura! Holy gee."

The train stops. He drags me out, pushes me against a marble pillar, and leans over. His breath makes me want to puke.

"Surprise!" He is swaying, drunk, always drunk, the degree of his drunkenness varied in accordance to available funds. "Look at you, you got fat."

Fat off your dick, asshole.

I wait for the opportune moment.

"Vova says you work for him now. Whore." He tightens his grip.

I wince.

Can I have it? says the eaglet.

In a moment.

It's hurting you.

I don't mind, I'm used to it. I don't want to spook it. When hunting a boar you don't attack it until you're sure of your aim. I'll hurt it back, eaglet, you'll see.

Okay, but please hurry.

The train departs. The platform is relatively empty.

"Your mother has cried herself sick." Lyosha spits.

You mean, drunk herself senseless?

"And here you are riding around metro. What did I tell you? What did I say I'd do if you run, you dumb bitch?" His voice drops. "You think because you rutted with Vova, you're his now? He's been asking me about you. Well, I told him you aren't his, you're mine. And you owe me my share." His hand flies up to slap me.

Now! says the eaglet.

I grip Lyosha's balls.

Rip them!

I twist and jerk down.

Lyosha's eyes bulge. For a second he is still and silent, then he erupts into a monstrous bellow and lets go of me, cradling his crotch. I stand next to him, watching him, mesmerized. His mug turns purple. He buckles and hollers. "You bitch! You will pay for this!" His cries drown in the rumble of the incoming train.

A small crowd gathers around us.

Go, go! says the eaglet.

I surface from my stupor and run.

Lyosha staggers after me.

I hear his footfalls and threats and curses. I weave through the crowd that streams along the vaulted vestibule in both directions and aim for the exit. My belly aches, my lungs are on fire, and I have to slow down.

I won't make it. I won't make it.

A train arrives on the opposite platform.

I take a deep breath and speed up, focusing on the escalators some twenty meters ahead. Lyosha gains on me. My muscles cramp and burn from exertion.

The train! says the eaglet. *Board the train!*

I lurch to my right, slip on the polished floor and almost fall. The train is about to depart.

"Be careful," says the voice, "the doors are closing. The next stop is—"

I know the recording by heart. I have a few seconds to make it.

Lyosha's hand gets a hold of my backpack.

I shoot forward, leaving it in his grip.

"—Tsvetnoy Boulevard."

I leap and crash inside. The doors bang shut. I double over, gulping for air, forcing myself to straighten.

DO NOT LEAN is stenciled on the glass.

Lyosha stands behind it, so close that his breath fogs it up. He shakes my backpack and yells something. His eyeballs are about to pop from their sockets.

And I grin. *Eat that, fuckface. Eat that, you swine. You sack of shit. You degenerate pervert.*

Those balls tasted good, says the eaglet. *When can I have the rest?*

Soon. I flip Lyosha two birds and watch him grow smaller and smaller.

The train picks up speed and enters the tunnel.

For the rest of the ride, I'm in ecstasy. I don't feel my legs and I don't know how I can stand upright, and my wet shirt and jeans sticking to my skin don't bother me. I even don't mind the loss of my jacket, my backpack, and my disability certificate with it. It was worth it.

I totter out onto Medeleevskaya and hop up the worn steps of the crossover to the Novoslobodskaya station. My sneakers make squelching noises. I walk along the long white-washed cavern together with the horde of grim shuffling bodies. By the wall on the right are the usual metro fixtures. An Afghan war veteran, a twenty-something guy without legs, sits on a piece of cardboard and brays an army song. A fleshy middle-aged woman sells yellow press. A pensioner begs for money, a few crumpled rubles and coins in his earflap hat.

I grin at every one of them. *I taught that pig a lesson.*

I run down the stairs to the station that looks like a crypt decorated with illuminated pylons and walk onto the platform.

"Citizen Myshko!" I hear Lenin's voice.

I spin around.

"Ay-ay, citizen Myshko," says Lenin. He's part of the

stained glass ornament lit up from inside. He sits by the desk with a globe on it, a stack of papers in his hands. "You still haven't answered my question. What is your goal in life?"

To shut you up. To live to the day when you *will listen to* me *and not the other way around.*

"You must believe in the Soviet power. It will teach you how to speak. Do you doubt it, citizen Myshko?" He points at me with an admonishing finger.

The only thing I doubt is if you can stick it up your ass, because it might be too fat for your tight communist butthole.

I exit on Smolenskaya.

The downpour has stopped but it's still drizzling.

I rub my arms and stop by the vending kiosks. A shoe repair booth, a newsstand, and a cigarette stall. Passersby come up, study the displays, exchange their rubles for goods, and move on. The street bustles with cars and trucks and buses and exhaust and dampness.

I'll walk to the White House and from there I'll find my way to Pavlik. I put a hand on my stomach. *Thank you, eaglet.*

For what?

For egging me on.

No, says the eaglet, *thank you.*

For what?

For not aborting me.

Oh. I shudder. *I'm sorry.*

It's okay. Don't be. Every mother wants to murder her child at least once in her life. You're not the first one and you're not the last one.

If that is true, how are we different from animals?

You mean, how people are different from animals?

Yes.

They aren't.

They aren't?

They're worse. They think because they've learned how to walk upright and how to talk about morals that they're somehow better, but they aren't. They kill each other every day.

Animals kill, too.

For survival.

And people?

People do it out of fear.

But you want me to kill Lyosha.

No. I want the animal in you to slaughter the boar.

I shake my head. *Wait.*

I'm the animal, not the mouse. Let me out.

I hold my face.

I'm cold from standing outside for so long in damp clothes and I want to pee. I rub my face and cup my elbows and jog to warm up and to stop thinking. I go down into a pedestrian underpass that smells of vomit and come up on the other side of the street and weave in and out of back alleys.

It's getting dark. Streetlights whiz to life. *Let the animal out. Let the animal out.*

I climb up the granite steps to the Freedom Square, pass by the remnants of the barricade, and meander through the streets for another hour, groping inside my memory for landmarks. Buildings or roofs or anything I saw that might lead me. Then I see a peeling church. We definitely drove by it on the way to Pavlik's place. Behind it is a daycare, two dismal concrete blocks sandwiched together.

I hop over the fence and cross the yard, ignoring the

smoking boys on one of the verandas and pretending like I don't hear them call me names and jeer. On the other side of the fence I come to the boulevard that ends in the familiar parking lot lit by a weak streetlight. There is the elm, now almost bare, and among other cars is parked the model 9 Lada.

I found it.

The parking lot is situated across from the last entranceway into the five-story brick Khrushchovka and I decide to try it first but my bladder is burning.

I look around. The yard is empty. I squat behind a tree.

A fat old woman in a kerchief labors out of the front door. A black cocker spaniel tugs on the leash in her hand. It sniffs the air and swings its head with floppy ears in my direction and begins to bark.

"Be quiet, Nika," says the woman, and gives me a stern glance. "Damned homeless, pissing anywhere they want."

I wait for them to clear, so I can pull up my pants, and suddenly, I'm angry. Angry at being chilled to the bone and hungry and broke and alone. Angry at this dog and the woman's outburst, at the dreary building where Pavlik lives, at not knowing his apartment number. Angry at everything.

A crow croaks at me. I pick up a stone and throw it at it.

There! Is that the animal you want?

It takes off, screeching.

I walk up to the entrance. The coded lock is gutted. The door gives a creak. A foul odor hits my nostrils: rotting potatoes, soggy garbage. It's dim and cold like a crypt. There is no elevator, typical Khrushchovka—the prefabricated Soviet housing wonder.

Citizens, to reward you for your loyalty to the Communist Party, we will give you free apartments. The buildings have no insulation and no elevators but jogging up and down the stairs is good for your communist health. Sucks if you're an invalid. Not our problem.

I think about the Afghan veteran I saw in the metro underpass.

I get your Soviet power, Lenin. Those who don't fit your ideals and who don't believe your dogmas are ostracized and then discarded, good as dead.

A hand brushes my ankle.

I flinch.

On the first floor landing lies a filthy drunk.

"Daughter. Help me."

I offer him a hand.

He slaps it. "No. Rubles. Give me rubles!"

An empty bottle of vodka rolls away from him, his crotch is wet. I edge around and sprint upstairs.

I press my ear to every door and listen. There are sounds of TV and Vysotsky songs. A couple has a fight, a baby cries, a dog is woofing. Most flats are quiet. I keep going until I reach the fifth floor. The second door on the left is the cleanest in the whole entranceway, newly painted metal with a shiny plastic number 18 above the spy-hole.

I smell meat dumplings. *This must be it.*

My heart drums hard. My stomach rumbles. I place my ear against the metal. Soft voices, clinking cutlery, then footsteps and a cough so close that I recoil.

"Yulechka, I'll go take out the trash."

The door chain jangles, the locks rasp and turn.

CHAPTER TEN

VIPER

I skid down three flights of stairs and cling to the garbage chute, faint with panic. DON'T THROW BURNING MATCHES AND CIGARETTES INTO THE GARBAGE CHUTE is stenciled on the shaft in big letters. The receptacle shutter yawns open. Rank odor issues from its depth. I retch. Puppies. Dead puppies. Grandma used to throw them down the chute after she drowned them in a bucket of freezing water.

The flapping of slippers above. The groan of rusty hinges and the echo of the garbage thudding past me and then a crash somewhere below. Slippers walk up and the door bangs shut.

I wait for a couple of minutes, then ascend and ring the bell.

An eye peers into the spy-hole.

I brush my bangs aside and smile.

Locks click and the door opens to the length of the chain. There's a warm smell of food, and then Yulia's unblinking eye studies me as if she hasn't seen me before.

"Excuse me, but who are you?"

I go through the pantomime.

"Ah, you're that girl from the hospital." She talks so quietly I can barely hear her.

I nod.

"Well, this is unexpected. Has Pavlik invited you?"

I shake my head.

"No? Then why did you come? And how do you know our address?"

"Mama, who is it?" says Pavlik from inside the apartment.

My face heats up. I hate it but I can't stop it and I'm blushing.

"It's the neighbor, Tatiana," says Yulia over her shoulder. "Asking for butter." She turns her unblinking eye at me. "What do you want?"

My backpack is gone and with it my notepad and pen. I take a step forward.

She shuts the door to a crack. "Don't come closer. Stay where you are."

Anton's voice says from behind her, "Who is it?"

"It's that mute girl from the hospital."

"She probably came to visit Pavlusha." There is an interest in his voice that I don't understand.

"But how does she know our address?"

"Well, they work together."

"So? How do we know she's not a scam artist?"

"Yulechka, calm down. Pavlusha said—"

"Pavlusha likes to tell stories."

"What is going on?" It's Pavlik's voice again. "Mama, who are you talking to?"

"Oh, it's nothing, nothing." Yulia shuts the door.

My heart cracks over the concrete floor. I stand like this for a few minutes, lost and unsure about what to do. Then the chain rattles and the door opens.

It takes me a moment before I can lift my head.

Pavlik leans on a pair of crutches, peaked, alert, and impeccably dressed. Black sweater over a light-blue shirt, jeans, and brown leather slippers.

"Irina!" His eyes light up. "How did you find me? Please, come in. I'm so happy to see you."

Are you? My stomach lurches.

"I'm sorry we left in a hurry, Papa had to—" He frowns. "Why aren't you wearing a jacket? You're freezing!"

He gently pushes me in.

It's so warm that my fingers tingle. The small narrow hallway and what I can glimpse of the parlor is spotless and organized to precision. Everything looks new and expensive. Embossed wallpaper, polished mahogany furniture, Turkish rugs, satin lampshades, and Gzhel plates on the wall.

I could eat off the floor here.

In the door to the parlor stands Anton in a coarse wool sweater, and next to him Yulia is in a green dress, her arms crossed and her face a mask of politeness.

"Irina, is that right?" she says.

I nod.

"Well, Irina. I'd like for you to explain to us the goal of your unexpected visit. Pavlusha, can you bring my notebook and pen from the kitchen?"

"Mama, please."

"Yulechka, they're friends. It's natural for friends to visit each other, don't you think?" Anton's smile is forced.

"Natural. Since when is visiting people unannounced natural? She could've at least called and warned us in advance. We had to interrupt our dinner."

"But how could she call? She doesn't talk! Pavlusha said—"

"I know what Pavlusha said, you don't need to remind me." Her unblinking eyes scorch me. "How old are you?"

I show with my fingers.

"Sixteen? And you're wandering alone, at night, after all this shooting? Do your parents know you're here?"

My parents? I smirk. *Well, my papa ditched me before I was born and I have no idea where he is. My mama is drunk most of the time, and Lyosha Kabansky, her current boyfriend, is no parent to me because he raped me every night for over a year. So no, my parents don't know I'm here because they don't give a shit about where I am or whether I'm alive or dead.*

"Mama, how about we continue at the table?" Pavlik grimaces. "It's uncomfortable for me to stand on the crutches for so long."

"Are you sure about this?"

"What do you mean?"

"You didn't complain once this morning when we were buying you clothes." She spins on her heel and enters the kitchen. Anton follows.

I let out compressed air. *Never mind my folks. At least they stab in the open.*

Pavlik's grimace is gone. "Do you like dumplings?"

I could eat a fried snake right now. Hell, I could eat one raw.

He points to the wardrobe. "There should be extra slippers in there." He says something else, but I don't hear it.

Suddenly, I'm wary. The warmth around me melts the

polished surfaces to sticky glue. I know that if I take a step I will get stuck here like a helpless mouse in a viper's lair.

Come on, Irina Myshko, it's what you wanted. It's better than the boar's shithole, is it not?

Pavlik gives me a pair of Yulia's slippers and I put them on.

I stay at Pavlik's place for two months.

He convinces his parents that my company is therapeutic and that I help him heal faster. Anton agrees on the account of life debt that needs to be repaid and I can see that it makes him feel good about himself for providing charity to a mute homeless girl. Yulia at first is reluctant and suspicious, then gets impressed with my mopping and scrubbing and cleaning. She even sends me grocery shopping.

I sleep on a mattress on the floor in the kitchen and it's the first time I have had my own room. It's packed with food, the perfect mouse cage.

Rain has long given way to snow. It covers dirt and coats Moscow with a white blanket.

I slowly gain weight. My breasts swell up and my belly bulbs out and I'm terrified to death of being discovered, dressing in layers of Yulia's hand-me-downs. Nobody has noticed a thing except Pavlik.

He gives me wondering looks but keeps mum.

It's the first Saturday of December. I've felt Pavlik's stares since he woke up and I sense he's going to ask me today.

We're eating breakfast alone in the kitchen. Yulia and Anton have gone to prepare their store for some jewelry exhibition. Behind the window, snowbanks glisten in the sun, their slopes bored with yellow doggy pissholes. Pedestrians wade through slush strewn with salt by the snowblowers.

The clock strikes ten.

I sip tea, waiting.

Pavlik sits across the table in the dappled shadow, his eyes distant. He forks up the last of the sunny-side up egg and finishes his coffee. There are no crutches leaning at the wall by his side, gone since last week. He gets up.

"Coming?"

Always.

I follow him to the heated covered balcony the width and the length of a daybed. Pine walls, a folding table, padded stools, cardboard boxes in the corner, and a pulley clothesline under the ceiling.

Pavlik cracks open the window. Freezing air drifts in.

My skin erupts in goose bumps.

He pulls out a pack of Davidoff's from his secret stash behind a loose panel, lights a cigarette, and takes a drag. It's been two months since Kostya's funeral and since he started smoking, but he's still awkward with it, holding the cigarette like a spoon. He puffs out ringlets of smoke and coughs.

There is no wind, only frigid sunshine. The inner court is spread below us like a bleached hanky.

"So," he says to the ground, "I wanted to ask you something. If you don't mind."

I think I know what it is. I sit on a stool next to him. My shoulder touches his thigh and I don't dare to breathe or to move. I want to press closer.

"Listen," he says, "you can't hide it forever, you know. Look, it's already—oh, dammit, it's not how I wanted to tell you. I'm sorry."

I look up.

His hand is in his hair. "Irina, I know you're pregnant."

I know that you know and I know that I'm suffering from denial. But for once, I'm so comfortable that I don't want to dredge up the past, to be reminded of him for as long as I can. Is that so bad?

"Irina."

I know I'm sitting in shit, okay? And if you stir it, it will stink and spoil everything. Please, it's such a nice morning.

"I talked to mama yesterday." He looks away.

I get cold all over.

"I think she suspects something. We can't continue pretending like it's not there. At some point, you'll get too large to hide it and then what? How will you explain it, tell them you have a hernia?"

I curl and uncurl my fists. *A hernia sounds about right.*

"This is what I don't understand. Why did you go to the hospital for an abortion if you knew you wouldn't go through with it?" He flicks out the stub and pulls up a stool and sits next to me.

"Why did you keep it?"

Do you really want to know?

He takes my hands. "Can I ask who the father is?"

There is no father, there is only the boar.

"Look, I'm sorry if I seem too forward about this. I couldn't help but notice how you sometimes look at your stomach and touch it and all these layers you wear and how you stoop on purpose and, well, it was easy to figure it out from there. I called the hospital to confirm. I'm sorry. I promise I won't tell anyone. Please. I just want to help. In case you wanted to talk."

Talk, I want to laugh. *I've forgotten how to want it.*

"Whatever it is, you can tell me. It'll die with me. I promise."

Don't say it.

His face hardens. "And I wish you'd stop giving yourself bruises. Yes, I've noticed." He tugs at his hair. "Please, Irina. I wouldn't be sitting here talking to you if not for you, don't you understand? I wish I could help you somehow in return, don't you get it?"

I shrink.

In the next moment he holds me and puts his cheek on mine and rocks me a little. My heart drums in my ears. I wanted this for so long, that now that it's happening I can't move.

And I know I'm in love.

Dura. Mute, stupid, dura. He said there is nothing between you, don't you remember?

But it's too late.

I don't care anymore. I just love him.

"Something wrong?" Pavlik lets go.

My face is wet. *Everything?*

He frowns. "Did I hurt you?"

Hurt me? No, I hurt myself.

He pulls out another cigarette. His hand shakes. "Can I ask something else?"

I wipe my face with a sleeve and nod.

Outside kids call to each other. A dog barks.

"I know you've explained it before, but...why is it that you don't talk? I mean, what's the real reason? I don't believe that you have a disability. Did something happen? Something that made you mute?"

I stare at the knots in the pine paneling.

He pulls out a notebook and a pen from under the stool. "Please?"

I flip through crinkly pages filled with my crooked writing—empty, elusive answers to his questions. I find a clean sheet and hold the pen to the paper, the tip almost touching it.

Okay. After this, I'll know if you really care.

CHAPTER ELEVEN

EELS

The words don't want to come. They resist the paper as if they don't belong there, as if they can only live inside my head. Every letter is a struggle. The pen and the notebook repel each other like the same ends of two magnets. I begin to sweat. *It's one thing that I can't talk, but now I can't write either?* It gets me angry and it breaks the resistance and I write.

I start with: "No one knows."

"No one knows what?" Pavlik reads over my shoulder.

"I haven't told anyone why I don't talk."

"No one at all?"

I shake my head. It's so easy, to shake my head, to nod, a convenient habit. I'm mad at it, and at my tongue that won't move, and at my shaking hands.

"Thank you," he says. "For sharing it with me."

Thank you? I gape at him. *For what? In a moment you won't thank me any longer.*

My heart thunders. I grip the pen to keep it rooted to the page. "I don't talk"—I write—"because the catfish made me not to."

"What?" His brows knit. He reads and rereads my words, his face close to mine. I smell his skin and see his lips moving. Then he pulls away and studies me for a minute.

A crow screeches, another one answers it. It sounds as if they're fighting for a scrap of food.

I wait, my stomach in knots.

You'll either tell me that I'm making fun of you or that I'm mental and need to be seen by a doctor or laugh it off as a bad joke or—

"Why?" he says with a strange light in his eyes. "What did you do to it? To the catfish?"

I gawk. There is no ridicule in his tone, no scorn. He fumbles with a cigarette, breaks it, and pulls out another.

I take a breath, then write, "I called it a bad word."

"What bad word?"

"Dura."

He chuckles. "There are worse words than that."

"It was bad enough."

"So what did it do?"

"It beat me into a mouse. Mice don't talk."

"Mouse? You're a mouse?"

"Yes." I want to drop the notebook and the pen and hide.

"And who is the catfish, if you don't mind me asking?"

"My mama."

"Does the catfish know"—he hesitates—"who the father—"

"No."

86

"Does...the mouse know?"

"Yes."

"Who is it?"

"The boar."

"The boar?" He drops the cigarette, picks it up. "Do the catfish and the boar know each other?" His every word is measured, careful.

"They live together, if you can call it living."

His hand touches my shoulder. "Does the boar know?"

"No."

"What did it do to the mouse?"

"It ate it. Tail to neck. Every night for a year."

"Is that why the mouse went to the hospital? Because the boar hurt it?"

"No, that was horseflies."

"Horseflies." He looks at the window and through it, as if it doesn't exist. "How many?"

"Five."

"Did they...bite the mouse?"

"Yes. Worse than the jackal." I don't know why I write it and I scratch it out but he stops my hand. "Wait. There was a jackal?"

"The one from the Chamber Theater."

Pavlik is still for a couple of seconds. Then his eyes narrow. "That scum. And I thought they were empty rumors about why Lida left. Did it bite you?"

"Only a handful of times. It's old. Its teeth are dull."

My throat spasms, my chest hurts, and my mouth tastes cruddy. The beasts want out and I write about every one of them. The cockroach, the herrings, the Lenin statue killing the woodpeckers, the tapeworm, the roosters, the turtle in the theater, the seal and the parrots, the mole and the sheep, the vultures, and the walrus. I write and write and write until my hand cramps.

The street is quiet. It's evening. The pine slats are rosy in the setting sun.

Pavlik throws his fifth or sixth cigarette stub out of the window. "I have a story, too."

I put the pen down.

"Nobody knows about this except my parents." His voice is muffled. "It happened at the old place where we lived, before we moved here. I was seven." He lights another cigarette. "I was walking home from school one night, around six in the evening, if I remember right. It was December, like now, dark and cold. I should've known better. Should've gone straight home but that little shit Mishka hid my schoolbag behind the trash bins and it took me hours to find it. I was afraid mama would scold me if I came home without my bag. So I went to the alley—to get to our building block you had to go through an unlit park—and there they were." He stops, eyes unfocused.

I feel his terror.

"Six of them." His pupils expand. "Six...eels. Swarthy, bristly, stoned out of their minds. They"—his face contorts with pain—"fell on me and burrowed in. One by one."

I take his hand. It's cold. He doesn't move, his cigarette forgotten.

"When they were done, they left me lying on the freezing ground. I remember I was looking at the stars in the night sky like they were beads of ice scattered on black velvet and I thought, this is it. I'm dying." There is water in his eyes. He quickly wipes it.

I can't breathe. *I'm sorry. I'm so sorry.*

I let go of his hand and scribble. "One of the vultures shot the macaw in the parking lot by your house. I saw it."

"What?" says Pavlik, startled. "The vulture what?"

"It was on the roof. It fired at the macaw and the butterfly."

"The macaw and the butterfly?" He sounds lost.

"The black admiral. It lived, but the macaw died. The mouse pushed the butterfly out of the way but it wasn't fast enough—"

Pavlik covers his face.

I toss the notebook and forget myself and hold him.

He sags into my arms and his hair is so close, so shiny and curly, that I pass my fingers through it. It's silky just like I expected. I sway from side to side, and he silently sheds tears into my sweater. We sit like this for a long time.

It's very dark. I can't see my hands. Bright light flares on and blinds me. I blink. From the parlor someone is knocking on the glass of the balcony door.

Pavlik stirs.

I see Yulia's face, stern, her eyebrows arched in wonder, and Anton's lips stretched in a grin.

We're still holding each other.

I jump up so fast, the edge of my sweater lifts to my bare skin and—

Shit!

She looks and she sees.

I hastily tug it down and smooth it over. My face is boiling and every bit of me is shaking.

"Hey." Pavlik opens the door. "Sorry. We lost track of time. Mama, are you okay?"

Her eyes fix on my waist and she throws a hand over her

mouth.

"Yulechka, what's the matter?" says Anton.

She points at my stomach as though she wants to poke it and watch it deflate. "This..." It's all she can manage. "This..."

I try to look innocent but the damage is done.

"What is it?" Anton follows her finger.

"You guys hungry?" Pavlik is trying to avert it. "How about some dinner? We've been sitting here all day."

"Pregnant," says Yulia. "She's pregnant!"

"She what?" Anton blinks.

"Can we please come inside? Thanks." Pavlik steps over the threshold and pulls me behind him. My legs turn to water.

Yulia's arms cross over her chest. She starts without preamble, already controlled. "How long has this been going on?" Her voice quavers slightly.

I'd prefer it if you yelled, you egocentric hypocrite. Be honest and say it to my face. Say you hate me. Say you want your son to be rich and famous, married to a girl who can shit diamonds and not some knocked up mute dura without a ruble to her name. Go ahead, say it. Say it! I grit my teeth.

"What are you talking about?" says Anton.

"She's pregnant! Can't you see?"

"Pregnant? Surely you don't think—" He shifts his gaze to Pavlik.

"What, you consider me incapable in that regard, Papa?"

Oh no. Oh no. Don't. I tug on Pavlik's sleeve.

He brushes me off.

"Watch your tone, son."

"I'm sorry, what is it exactly that you want me to watch?" Pavlik's voice is high, unnatural.

"All this time, right under my nose." Yulia pins him with a burning stare. "You never had any secrets from me, Pavlusha, you always told me everything. Why?"

No! I seize Pavlik's hand. He roughly twists it out.

"Us," says Anton. "Told us everything."

Yulia's skin attains a shade of green. "This is how you repay us? For everything we've done for you? This is what you do?"

Pavlik's face is working and it doesn't look good.

I wave my arms, *it's not his, it's not his,* and step to the balcony to get the notebook, but Pavlik blocks me.

I'm so surprised that I back away and sink into the sofa and stare at the mahogany console draped with a crocheted hanky, the TV sitting on top of it. Unfeeling, unhearing. It's over, it's all over.

Good job, Irina Myshko. Get ready to be kicked out. Where will you go now? In the middle of winter? Pregnant? What will you eat, where will you sleep? Whose ass will you kiss to make them take you in?

"Mama, Papa, please. Calm down. There is no need for this hostility. I can—"

"Hostility?" Yulia inflates. "Hostility? I almost lost you once and you're talking to me about hostility?" She looks at her husband. "Don't be quiet. Say something."

"Of course, Yulechka, of course." He grills me through his thick glasses. "Irina, tell us. Are you, in fact, pregnant?"

Their eyes are on me.

I shrink into the sofa.

"Why are you asking her? Like she'll admit to it." Yulia is livid. "You tricked us, you lied to us. You coerced my son into an affair. After everything we went through with him, all these years of pain and suffering, you come and, in the matter of months, you wreck his future. We trusted you, we took you in, fed you, clothed you. And you—" She catches her breath, veins prominent on her neck. "You trash! You—"

"Mama, stop it!"

No, let her. I get up from the sofa, seething. *She's finally telling me what she really thinks.*

"How dare you yell at your mother!"

"The same as she dares to yell at Irina!"

"Pull up your sweater, please," says Yulia.

I automatically cradle my belly in a protective hold and it jolts. The baby inside me moves. A faint passing feeling like a shift or a touch or a fluttering of wings. I look down and it does it again. The sensation of something floating, almost ticklish.

Eaglet?

I gaze up, my mind blank.

They are arguing and shaking fingers and Yulia is reaching over to me and Anton has froth around his mouth and Pavlik stops them both with his hands up and intercepts my stare and his eyes go wild and I know what he's about to do but I can't move.

He passes compressed air between his lips and I hear him say it. "That's enough of that. You're making my head hurt. It's my life and my baby. Our baby. If you want no part of it, it's your choice. We'll figure things out on our own."

What are you doing, Pavlik?

"We raised you," says Yulia, suddenly teary. "We got you into one of the most prestigious Moscow schools, we're paying your way through theater, bending over backward for Simeon Ignatievich to advance your career, and you go and lie with some trash. You're a child, Pavlusha. You're only eighteen. Don't you understand what this will do to you? It will ruin your life."

"What do you know about bending over backward?"

Yulia goes pale. "You mustn't say it. Don't say it."

"Why not?"

"This is why you were so adamant she stayed. This is why

you brought her here, for us to get used to her. You planned it all along, am I right? You counted on us to raise your child while you two skip onstage, having the time of your lives. Well, I won't have it, Pavlusha. Over my dead body."

"Then we will leave."

They face each other.

The baby moves again, as if it wants me to notice.

I've felt you, eaglet, I've felt you!

Yulia pushes Pavlik out of the way and slaps me and—

The mouse squeaks. The owl hoots and the viper hisses. They scare off the butterfly and descend on the mouse. Prod it, poke it, flip it over, and jab its belly. The mouse feels the eaglet eddy in its stomach, wanting to get out, to become a grown bird, a savage predator that can kill the viper and the owl and the boar and any beast that dares to hurt it.

The mouse peeps, content. It will let the eagle out even if that means it will destroy the mouse in the process.

CHAPTER TWELVE

BUTTERFLY

A door slam breaks my slumber. I surface and sit up. It's night. I'm on Pavlik's creaky bed draped with a handwoven carpet. The table lamp throws a ring of light on the desk. His jean jacket is draped over the back of the chair. Posters hang on the wall: Sim, Kostya, some other actors I don't know. His backpack on the Turkish rug, a stack of books. Everything is neat and clean and organized. The last time I was here it was after Kostya's funeral.

My stomach churns and I reel.

Pavlik stands next to me. I catch his scent of pollen and bitter flower dust. His hair is ruffled and his eyes are grim and reckless as if he's set on something dangerous.

"Are you feeling any better?"

I sense it's not what he wants to say and wait.

"You know what?" He throws up his arms and slaps his thighs. "I told them to leave us alone. Don't know about you, but I'm done. And I don't want you sleeping in the kitchen anymore. Take my bed. I'll sleep on the floor."

He pulls his turtleneck over his head and throws it on the chair. Next goes the muscle shirt, jeans, and socks. All that's left are cotton briefs, starkly white in the semi-darkness. He looks around in search of something. I tense and relax and tense and pulse and throb. Blood fills my head. I stare at him, milky from the lack of sun but not deathly pale. Lucid. I become aware of my fingers. They tingle. I want to touch his skin like I touched his hair on the balcony.

What if he pushes me away?

And I know.

I unbutton my shirt.

Pavlik takes out a rolled up mattress from the wardrobe, unrolls it on the floor by the bed, and shakes out a folded checkered woolen blanket.

While he is searching for spare bedding I strip naked and recline on the pillow, trembling from anticipation. I've never given myself away freely before, I was always taken. This is my first time and I want Pavlik to do it. I open my legs and wait.

Take me. Please, take me.

Pavlik closes the wardrobe, turns around and drops the sheets. A strange noise escapes him. "Yeek." He stares at my thighs, then at my face.

My every nerve is on fire. I gather the blanket into fists, willing myself not to groan.

Why aren't you taking me?

He's transfixed. "Irina, what are you doing?"

I want you to have me. Take me. I love you.

He picks up the sheet and carefully covers me with it up to

my chin.

I throw it off, bewildered. *What's wrong? Why don't you want me? Am I too fat? Too ugly? Too dumb? Are you afraid to hurt the baby? Do my bruises disgust you? What?*

He gives me a wan smile and sits on the edge of the bed. Old springs whine. He touches my face, gingerly, like it might break in his hold.

"You're beautiful, you know that?"

Are you shy? Wait, are you a virgin? I cup the bulge in his briefs. It's limp.

Pavlik moves my hand away. "Please, don't. I'd prefer it if you didn't touch it."

I'm confused.

"It's not that you're not lovely, you are. It's just that, only Kostya was allowed to touch it." He lowers his eyes.

My ears ring. *What? Kostya?*

It dawns on me and chills me to the bone and makes me brittle. One touch and I will break. *The macaw and the butterfly. How could I be so blind?*

Pavlik's silhouette is lost in the shadow. "Irina."

I see him and I don't. He is one with the night, with the darkness in the room. Black like the wings of the black admiral.

He lets out his breath. "I'm gay."

There is the ticking of the clock and the empty silence that fills me with a void. I'm blank and hollow.

"Kostya and I, we were seeing each other." He pauses. "My parents have no idea. Please don't tell them, it will devastate them. Promise me you won't."

I don't know how, my neck is so stiff, but I nod.

He leans on me then. I wrap him in the blanket as best as I can and place him in my lap until he cries it all out and falls asleep. I get numb from sitting without moving, and soon after him, I doze off.

The crying of the crows wakes me. The clock on the desk shows five after six. The early morning light colors the room dusty blue, like the ghost of the macaw.

Long shadows trace Pavlik's face. He snores lightly. It takes me a long time to slide out from under him. It's chilly and my skin crawls with goose bumps. I pick up my clothes from the rug and dress, and stand over him, watching him breathe.

It makes sense now. Your polite interest in my life and your polished mannerisms and your gratitude, nothing more than a thin veneer. And Kostya. His distaste for me, a girl, a peasant girl, an abominable creature. The hours you spent together, rehearsing and not rehearsing.

I scribble on the notebook and tap Pavlik's shoulder.

"Please, don't." He turns away.

I shake him.

"Please. I'm trying to sleep." He covers his head with the blanket.

I persist until he jerks up. "What? What time is it?"

I show him the notebook. "Why did you say it's your baby?"

"Oh, this." He yawns and rubs his face. "Well, you saved my life and I wanted to return the favor." He sounds pragmatic and irritated, like his father.

I slap the page. "Liar."

He hangs his head.

"That's not the real reason."

"Yes, you're right, you're right. It's not. I can't hide anything from you, you're so perceptive." He looks beaten. "What do you want me to say?"

I wait, immobile. Behind the window crows croak as if they're talking to each other.

"Okay. The truth is"—he glances at the door—"Papa has suspected me for some time now, and, well, this was the perfect opportunity to prove him wrong. He never really liked Kostya. All that time we spent together. And he doesn't like it that I use makeup at the theater, he doesn't think it's manly. He used to drill me about not having a girlfriend. It's gotten to the point where I started avoiding him. Then you showed up. So he finally got off my back. And when I found out that you're pregnant, I thought it would be a perfect opportunity to secure his belief—"

I throw the notebook at the wall. It smacks and drops to the floor in a heap of rustling pages.

Nice, Irina Myshko. You've been used again. What is wrong with you? You just don't learn, do you?

"Please, don't be mad. I'm sorry. I really am. I should've asked you first, I know. I'm such an idiot." He reaches out, arms outstretched.

Yesterday it would've sent my heart aflutter. Now it jars me. I edge away. *I'm just a tool for you, to solve your petty problems. I've been nothing but a tool for men all of my life.*

I pick up the notepad and write. "Why?"

"Why what?" His face is lifeless.

"Why did you ask me why I'm mute?"

"Oh. I don't know. I guess I wanted to help." He suddenly smiles. "You got me at first. I thought, catfish? What catfish? It took me a moment."

I want to claw the smile off his face.

He notices my expression and becomes serious. "No one has listened to you before, have they?"

I grit my teeth.

"In a way you made it easier for me to share." He pauses. "Eels. They really did look like eels."

"You don't love me," I write.

"No-no. Of course I do. I do love you. Just not in the sense of how a man loves a woman. You're like a friend to me, a very dear friend, like a sister." He falls silent. "Do you love me?"

I turn away.

You're all the same—gay, straight, doesn't matter. I thought I'd found the one. No such thing.

The next words are the hardest to write. "What if I don't want you to be the father of my baby?"

"You don't? But I assumed..."

You assumed? My breath rattles. *I'm nothing but a victim, a lab mouse to practice your pity and compassion on.* I seize the doorknob.

"Don't go."

I face him. *Maybe it's for the best that they found out; maybe it's not my place to be here, in this shiny cage. Maybe I should go home, where I belong, in a shithole.*

I shake off his hand and yank the door open and crash through the parlor past sleeping Yulia and Anton. I step into the hand-me-down boots, throw on the coat, and bustle out, down the stairs and into the fresh-crunching snow.

Frost hits my face. It must be about minus-twenty degrees Celsius.

In front of me on the sidewalk shifts and squirms a dark mass of feathers. A pack of crows nibbles on a dead dog, frozen stiff, its eyes gone and its belly torn open. I recognize it. It's the black cocker spaniel, Nika, that belongs to the old fat woman from the first floor. It looks as if it's been run over by a car.

I stomp.

The crows scatter, cawing madly. I hasten across the street

to the parking lot. Steam puffs out of my nostrils and my nose hairs stick together when I inhale and my ears ache from the frost. I forgot a hat. I don't mind. All I want is to get away, to breathe, to think, and to decide what to do next.

The crows screech and hop after me, goading. One of them, the biggest and the blackest, swoops so closely that I feel the rush of air on my face and hear the swish of feathers. It circles, dives, and goes for another pass.

I shoo it away.

It lands on the elm and sets its beady eyes on me.

My skin crawls. *Your plumage is so glossy, your bills are curved, and the way you cry, hoarse and low. You're not crows, you're ravens.*

As if they heard me, they answer in indignant croaks and congregate around the dog and rip out strips of frozen meat.

The raven on the elm keeps watching me.

I feel uneasy. Deep in my gut I know something is wrong, but I don't know what.

I'm just paranoid.

I step into the fresh snow that fell in the night and hook one foot at a right angle to the nook of the other, and walk forward making a pattern like that from the tire of a large truck. I finish at the other end of the parking lot and kneel and scoop up a handful of snow and look at it, at how peaceful it is, how soft and smooth and white.

Why can't my life be like this? Why does it always have to turn upside down just when I think I got lucky?

Crunching footfalls.

I start.

About ten guys in black coats and black caps pour out of Pavlik's entranceway and slap each other's backs, croaking.

Like ravens.

I frown. I've never seen them before. They don't live here.

I wait until they're out of sight and run in, shivering, stomping off the snow. My ears and fingers burn. Voices echo up and down the stairs. A mother and a little girl bundled up to her nose pass me. Somewhere above a door bangs. I rub my hands and search for any sign of anything unusual. I find nothing, but the feeling won't leave me. The feeling that it has something to do with Pavlik.

I hurry to the last floor and fit the key into the hole and creep in.

CHAPTER THIRTEEN

DONKEYS

I peel off the coat and smell oatmeal. Noises come from the kitchen: the scraping spoons, the boiling kettle, and the morning news. *Great, I woke them up. No chance of talking to Pavlik now.* I kick off the boots, glance in the mirror, smooth my bangs, and walk in the parlor. The bed is folded back into the sofa. Pavlik's door is closed. I enter the kitchen. The clock shows a quarter to eight. A bored newscaster rattles on the screen, and below it, in the circle of light, Yulia and Anton hunch over breakfast.

Did he fall back asleep as if nothing happened?

I stand in the bubble of silent tension, deliberately unnoticed after yesterday's drama.

Anton reads the paper, a bowl of half-eaten porridge and a cup of coffee in front of him. He peers at me through his glasses

102

and goes back to reading without a word. Yulia bites into a buttered roll and scans a magazine. Like I'm not there, like I don't exist. She chews, swallows, and takes a sip from her cup.

"We're going to a gynecologist, you and I." Her voice is acid. "I'm not sure when yet, but soon." She looks up.

Gynecologist? To confirm that Pavlik is the father? The thought chills me. *Didn't you want to leave for home an hour ago, Irina Myshko?*

"And I'd appreciate it if in the future you didn't slam a door at six in the morning. It's unacceptable in our house." She makes an emphasis on *our house.* "Get ready, please. Simeon Ignatievich is picking both of you up"—she glances at the clock—"any minute now."

Sim?

"To celebrate the beginning of a new family, Irina. You remember Simeon Ignatievich, right? The Chamber Theater director?"

How does he know?

"Now," she says, leaning toward me, "do me a favor. Please, don't do anything stupid. Smile, nod, and stay quiet, like you always do. This meeting is very important for Pavlusha's career."

Like I always do. Mute, always accepting, always agreeable.

Anton sets his cup on the saucer with a clink. His eyes latch on me. "Please," he says. "We're both asking you. Nothing stupid."

Ten minutes later, we're dressed and making our way outside.

Pavlik's face is grim and silent. I want to ask if this was arranged behind his back, if he was the one who told Sim, but the trace of a bad feeling interrupts me.

We're out the door and the snow on the curb, the spot

where the dead cocker spaniel lay, is empty save for a few clumps of hair and some brownish spots and claw marks.

Did someone move it? Did the ravens drag it off? They couldn't possibly be that strong. Could they?

I sense eyes on my back. Sharp, astute, and searching. I spin and there they are, perched on the edge of the roof. Ravens, close to a hundred. Their wings touch and their feathers ruffle on the breeze. They sit silently, goggling at me, as if they're planning mischief.

We're watching you, they seem to say.

My heart leaps to my throat and stays there.

Pavlik takes my hand.

Snow crunches under the wheels of a glossy golden Mercedes that rolls into the parking lot and stops. Out staggers a large figure sheathed in a wool coat and wrapped in a bright scarf.

"Good morning, children!"

"Morning, Sim," says Pavlik.

I wave.

We cross the street and walk into his arms. He gives us the embrace of authority, of a superior animal. His perfume is all around me, the salty crisp smell of sea.

"Congratulations! That's exciting news." He lets go forcefully, as if he wants to break us apart. He smiles but his eyes are resentful.

"Thank you," says Pavlik.

"Children, children. You're so young." He shakes his head. "Why didn't you tell me?"

Pavlik opens his mouth and closes it.

"What is it? Are you sick? Have you lost your voice?" Sim's words are cutting.

"I'm sorry." Pavlik forces a smile. "I'm still waking up."

"Are you? Well, this will wake you up in no time. Get in."
Sim slaps Pavlik's ass with a familiarity that doesn't leave space
for doubt. Like he's done it before and he'll do it again whenever
it pleases him.

Pavlik cringes.

Oh no, oh no, oh no. Everything inside of me breaks and
drops.

Sim intercepts my gaze. "What are you looking at? Get in,
Irina. We're going to the House of Actors."

I open the door and make my numb legs move, sinking
into the leather. It's warm and it smells of smoke and it reminds
me of Kostya's car.

Pavlik's lips touch my ear. "It's not what you think it is."

I understand. It's important for your career. I stare at my
hands in my lap and I try not to think, not to imagine, but I
can't help it.

We leave the boulevard and nose into traffic, crawling
toward Moscow center. I scan the buildings and the sky. It's
clear and blue. No crows, no vultures, only a few pigeons dot
the sidewalks, rumpled and frozen.

We stop at the red light.

Sim turns around and regards us. Pavlik, me, Pavlik again.
"What were you thinking with, your head or your cock?" His
smile is gone.

The light turns green. The car behind us honks.

"Sim, please," says Pavlik.

I feel his pain and his submission and I hate it. I want to
get out and run and stumble and fall and bury my flaming face
in the snow and forget.

Sim jerks the car forward. "This is simply beyond me. Beyond me."

Pavlik finds my hand. I clutch it.

"A baby." Sim snorts. "You're a child. She's a child. What were you thinking?"

My stomach hurts so bad I want to retch.

We turn into a narrow alley.

Peeling mansions, bleak cafes, a hair salon, a curtain store. No trees and hardly any people. Shouts ring ahead, roaring and braying. Then I see them.

A straggling rally led by a man dressed in a black military uniform with a black beret cocked to the side on his shaved head, a megaphone perched to his working mouth. A mob of men follows him. Their hair is also shaved or cropped very short and they have dumb pink faces. Some of them hold up red flags with a circled white swastika-like symbol in the middle, the one I saw on the portrait in Shakalov's office.

Suddenly I know who they are.

Donkeys. Nazi donkeys headed by a raven.

"What's this now?" Sim pushes on the breaks.

Within seconds they swoop the car, slapping the hood and the sides. A gangly kid lowers his face level with Pavlik's and spits. His saliva slips down the glass and leaves a slimy streak. He shouts something to his mates. Pavlik recoils. One of them straddles a flagpole and humps it. A couple more crowd the driver's window, holler at Sim, and ululate and flip him off.

Their calls become an audible chant.

"Homos out of Russia! Homos out of Russia!"

"Sim," says Pavlik.

Sim's face drains of color. He grips the wheel and doesn't move.

Hands ram into the car and shake it.

"Sim!" says Pavlik. "They'll break the car!"

"To hell with it. Let them. I feel sorry for them. Look at them, black with hate."

A militia siren whines in the distance and they scatter. Only their handprints are left on the glass.

Sim pulls up to the curb, parks and exits.

Pavlik holds the door open for me.

I get out and look up, past the windows of a Gothic concrete block, past a stone knight on a cornice, and I meet their avian stare. A throng of ravens perched on the roof.

Just you try. I'll find a way to break your necks.

They screech and take off.

Sim urges us through the oak doors to the elevator and we get out on the last floor, where famous actors and poets and theatergoers like to mingle. Eat, drink, and philosophize. Throw around pompous words and engage in empty polemic.

I pay no attention to the décor or the ambiance. I want to puke. I go through my pantomime and flee to the restroom at the end of the hallway. I turn on cold water and see myself in the mirror. Wild reddish eyes with circles underneath stare back at me, bitter thoughts drilling through my head.

Pavlik is gay. I scoop up a handful of water and splash it on my face.

Sim is gay. Another splash.

Pavlik and Kostya were seeing each other because they were in love. Water drips on my shirt. I keep splashing.

Sim is using Pavlik like Lyosha was using me.

The splashing is not enough. I dip my face under the faucet and let the stream run over it. I stand like this until my hands stop shaking and I can draw one uninterrupted breath.

What did you think, Irina Myshko? You thought there are those who have it better? You naïve dura.

I want to punch the sink and the mirror and the wall. The urge is so strong that I almost do it. Instead, I reach under my shirt, twist my skin, and add to my collection of bruises. Then I lean over the sink and cry for a long time.

Those donkey faces. The hostility in them, the rage, the madness. I blow my nose and wipe my face.

The women who come in give me strange looks. Older women, painted, polished, and jeweled. I wait for an empty stall, squat, do my business, and get out.

I meander through dinner halls and finally spot Sim and Pavlik in the smallest one, at a table in the corner by a piano. They don't see me, as they are bent over, deep in a heated argument, their faces red from the glow of the ruby-colored wallpaper and matching velvet chairs. Classic theater aura. The walls are hung with actors' portraits in heavy gilded frames. No other diners are present except a well-dressed middle-aged couple at a table by the window.

I make my way over to Sim and Pavlik and draw out a chair.

They abruptly fall silent.

Pavlik's eyes are puffy, as if he was crying.

"Irina! You're alive." Sim spreads his arms. "We thought maybe you'd eloped with the chef and left us alone." He says it cheerily but I detect malice in his tone, as if he really wants it to happen. He wants me out of here, out of Pavlik's life.

He gives me the menu. "Go ahead. We already ordered."

I'm hungry. Every dish name draws saliva. Then I read, WILD BOAR BRISKET. My finger stops on it.

Eaglet?

No answer.

Eaglet, talk to me.

Same silence and some breathing.

Listen, I'm sorry—

You promised, says the eaglet.

I know.

You promised me a whole boar. I only got a taste of it, and now you want to feed me some pig's brisket.

I'm sorry. I was going to—

No, you weren't. You got comfortable, lazy, and you forgot.

My cheeks burn. I have nothing to retort with.

Our food arrives. I tuck into the brisket and devour it in minutes and belch. Pavlik smirks at me, his first smile since this morning. I notice he is drinking. They both are. Sim downs vodka, shot after shot. He leans over the table and says to me hotly, "Pavlik's got a gorgeous cock, doesn't he?"

Pavlik chokes on his food. "Sim."

My mouth opens. *You're jealous. You're hurt and jealous like a little boy, drinking yourself stupid.*

"Tell me. Do you love him? Do you truly love him?"

Pavlik looks at me strangely.

I don't want to, but I automatically nod.

"Really." Sim's eyes are unfocused. His forehead is sweaty. "And what is it you love more, him or his cock?"

"Sim. You said you wouldn't—"

"Waiter!" Sim waves the empty shot glass.

"Please, no more." Pavlik touches Sim's arm. Sim picks up his hand and kisses it.

Pavlik jerks back. "Not here. There are people..."

A pimply waiter appears with a bottle of Stolichnaya.

Sim snatches it and pours himself a shot. The chair groans under his weight. "Ladies and gentlemen, I give you Pavel and Irina Baboch. To future parents!"

Pavlik says, "Irina, help me."

After paying, we heave Sim up by the armpits to help him stand, leading him to the elevator and out the oak doors into the cold and indifferent December sun. The sidewalk is covered with gray slush mixed by hundreds of feet.

On the hood of Sim's golden Mercedes sits a dark lump of

human excrement. It gives off a hideous stink.

I gag.

"Oh God," says Pavlik.

Sim sees it too. "Scum! Low, cowardly scum!"

Passersby shrink back and give us odd looks.

I kneel, and Pavlik joins me.

We scoop handfuls of snow from the curb and dump it on top of the turd, coating and patting around it so that we can fling it from the hood. It leaves a hideous smear. We wipe the hood with the snow until every trace of it is gone.

My hands are red and throbbing from the cold. I wipe them on my jacket and tuck them under my arms.

"Thank you, children." Sim fumbles with the keys, shaken and sober. "I feel sick. I need to go home and lie down."

Pavlik nudges me. "Coming?"

The moment I get in, the car tears into the street, swerving. I close my eyes and grip the door handle.

CHAPTER FOURTEEN

SEAL

The car stops. I step out. We're parked at the end of Tverskaya Avenue by an opulent neoclassical building that takes up a whole block. Its granite base is stuffed with boutiques. Above it are five marble stories with ornamental balconies and tall narrow windows. The street is full of cars and people and city noises and dusk. I look to the Red Square. Last sunrays gild the steeples of the Historical Museum and the lights come on and the enormous New Year's tree in front of it flares up—a five-point star on its tip and countless twinkling garlands.

It'll be New Year's soon. I'm almost seventeen and I still haven't seen the Kremlin New Year's Tree show, the only one where Uncle Frost is not drunk out of his mind for fear of being sacked. Dumb animal. All of them are. And I'm no different. I glorify my victimhood. For what? To justify my hate. I hate everyone and everything. Do you hear me? I hate you!

Let the animal out, says the eaglet.

I will.

And I flinch. Something is wrong. The din is gone, replaced by a ringing silence.

They're here, they have heard me. The beasts. The woodpeckers and the roosters and the maggots. They boil over the edges of every crevice and crawl out of every hole and advance at me. The sheep and the donkeys and the geese. Horseflies, clouds of horseflies, buzzing and shifting. Above them, circling vultures and ravens. A black army, a bird on every outcrop, on every post.

Let the animal out, they screech. *Who are you? We want to see.*

The ground shakes. There is a horrible splintering and crashing noise, like breaking bones. I spin around. The Historical Museum collapses in a pile of bricks and out rides a tank with Lenin standing in the open hatch, right arm outstretched, left in his trouser pocket. The steel chassis thunders across Manege Square to Tverskaya.

It's not a statue, it's his embalmed body from the Mausoleum.

"What animal are you, citizen Myshko?" he shouts, his sunken eyeballs two stones, his lips bloodless, his skin yellow cellophane stretched over his skull. The turret turns and points at me.

I'm dizzy with fear.

I'm a mouse. Am I? I don't know anymore.

My knees buckle.

Pavlik catches me and leads me under the archway to the entrance lobby in the back of the building. We enter an old-style ascending-room elevator, close the metal-grate doors, and ride to the last floor, stepping out into a carpeted corridor. Sim unlocks his apartment and beckons us in.

It's newly remodeled and must be very expensive. The sound of classical music comes from everywhere. Bells, trumpets, piano. The long hallway is hung with heavy frames. Paintings, mirrors, placards. A posh rug covers the polished parquet.

Sim throws his coat on the floor and the keys on the glass table littered with magazines, kicks off shoes, and vanishes through a doorway on the right.

"Tea? Coffee?" I hear running water, jangling silvery, and clinking cups.

"Coffee for me and Irina, please," says Pavlik, and then to me, "Where are you?"

I blink. *I don't know.*

"Jacket?" He helps me out of it, picks up Sim's coat, and hangs them in a wardrobe. His movements are swift and habitual.

"You're so pale. Come on." He takes my hand and pulls me into the kitchen.

It sparkles with chrome. Large windows with sills wide enough to sit on offer a stunning view of the busy Tverskaya Avenue. Bottles of liquor and packets of food litter every surface, some are open, some still sealed. Baguettes, ham, cheese, smoked fish, jars of wild mushrooms and jam and pickled cabbage. My stomach rumbles. I need to use the bathroom.

Sim hums to the music and works the elaborate brewing machine. The smell of fresh coffee fills the room.

"What's with the long faces? Smile, children, smile." He puts three steaming cups on the table.

"Smile? Sim, they shat on your car."

"Yes." He smacks the table with the flat of his hand. The coffee spills. "They've shat on me my entire life. Every step of the way. Do you think it has stopped me?" He stoops and flings his arms around us. "I want you to listen inside you. Lis-ten. What do you hear?"

"Music," says Pavlik flatly.

"That's right. And what creates it, that music?"

Pavlik glances at me, tired.

I sigh.

"Haven't I taught you anything? Love. Love is what creates it. They have no music. None. They envy us. No matter what they do, it mustn't stop you from making your art. Never, do you hear me?"

"Yes, Sim, I hear you."

"Ne-ver!"

I'm overwhelmed with aversion. *The genius director and his pet actor. The seal and the butterfly. He'll squish you and you won't even notice.*

"What if it escalates?" says Pavlik. "What if it's shit today, guns tomorrow?"

"You think I haven't been under a gun?" Sim lights a cigarette and cracks open the window. "Why, you're mistaken, my child. I've had worse happen to me, but we'll talk about it some other time. Right now, we will talk about Irina's pregnancy and your future. Your joint future."

I can't hold it anymore. I slide off the stool and pat my stomach to excuse myself, and walk to the end of the corridor and open a door.

It's the wrong room.

A large window behind lacy curtains, rows and rows of books in tall bookcases, a writing desk heaped with papers, a monitor, a keyboard. Cut crystal ashtrays packed with cigarette stubs. A leather sofa. Shoes and scarves thrown about the floor. I stand still, listen to a mechanical ticking.

I want to look out at the street, to see if the beasts are still there.

You know where you're headed, Irina Myshko, don't you? Once they find out, they'll stick you in that same mental clinic where they stick your mama every fall and every spring. They'll feed you drugs for a month then send you home to your dear Lyosha Kabansky, the boar with the sinewy dick that he'll shove up your—

Stop!

I totter out and barge through the door across the hall. It's the bathroom. I pee and wash my face and feel a little better. I steal back into the kitchen and halt.

Pavlik is propped up with his stomach against the counter, Sim spooning him from behind. His stubby ring-encrusted hand is massaging Pavlik's buttocks. From time to time it slides in between his thighs. Pavlik's eyes are closed. His face is rigid and his jaw is set, as though he's tolerating it. Sim rubs against him with little grunts and whispers something in his ear, the coffee cup forgotten on the windowsill.

I release a shuddering exhale.

Pavlik jerks to look.

Sim follows his gaze. "Irina! What's the matter?"

I storm out and run into the bathroom, sliding the latch into place.

You won't, you won't, you won't! But I can't keep them back. Hot tears splash on the ceramic tiles. I ram a fist into the sink. It hurts. I cry out, unbutton my shirt, seize a handful of skin and twist and pinch and tear.

A knock. "Irina?" Pavlik's voice. The knob rattles. "Can you please open the door?" He waits. "Please."

I'll never let anyone in, ever again. Never! Leave me alone! Go away! I hate you! I hate everyone! You all hurt each other for no reason!

Pavlik says something, but I don't hear him anymore—

The mouse sits on the wet floor. Something large hammers on the door and the latch groans and gives. Dust sprays in a chalky cloud. The door bangs open. A seal tumbles down next to the mouse and the butterfly flutters in after it. The mouse backs into a corner. The seal picks it up with its front flipper. The mouse bites it, and the seal roars and throws it at the wall and it drops to the floor. The butterfly flits about, useless. The seal scoops up the mouse and wriggles through an underpass into the night sprinkled with white snow flurries.

The mouse shivers from the cold. The butterfly clings to it, sluggish. They glide on ice in the company of other beasts. Lulled by the movement, the mouse yawns and slips off the seal's flipper onto something soft and warm, and falls asleep.

It dreams of ravens. They surround the butterfly and peck at it and stab it and—

"Irina?"

I rise to the surface.

"Wake up." A hand shakes me. "We've arrived."

My eyelids are heavy with slumber. I blink a couple of times and see Pavlik's face, pale in the shadows.

"How are you feeling? You passed out in the bathroom. We had to break open the door to get you."

I rub my face. I'm in the back of Sim's car. He's sitting in the driver's seat, half-turned.

"Are you awake?"

I nod.

"Good. I have something important to tell you."

I go cold.

"This pregnancy of yours—"

"What about it?" says Pavlik.

"Don't interrupt me. Irina, listen to me. I've known Pavlik for years, and I get what it is you're trying to do."

"Wait, wait. I don't understand—"

"Am I talking to you?"

"No."

"Then please keep your mouth shut." Sim's eyes glitter with annoyance. "Irina, this boy can't lift his precious cock unless another one is in his tight little butthole. He's as gay as they get."

"Sim!" Pavlik glares. "Stop it!"

"Calm down. You two will do each other a favor. I assume that whomever the father of the baby is, he either doesn't know about it or doesn't care, am I correct?"

I stare at my palms.

"I thought so. Well, here is what you will do. You will get married."

"Married?" Pavlik's voice cracks.

Married? Blood rushes to my head.

"What's with the surprised faces? There is nothing unusual about two young people getting married. You will get married, you'll have a baby, and people will think it's yours, Pavlik. It will protect you until you grow a thick enough hide to deal with that scum. Do you hear me?"

Pavlik is silent.

I can't seem to take a breath.

Someone yells in the street. Soft flops of snow start falling, hushing noises.

"Do you hear what I'm saying?"

"Yes," says Pavlik.

"Good. Now get out. I'm tired." He starts the car.

"Thanks for the ride."

We trot through the patter of snow into the warmth of the entranceway and I immediately feel the threat.

The ravens. I seize Pavlik's arm.

"What is it?"

The ravens and the jackal. It smells like them.

"We're almost home, you can—" He stops. "Oh, great. Look. Someone broke our mailbox."

On the wall hang four boxes with five slots each, painted sickly green and stenciled with apartment numbers. Some are bent, some dented, others charred. The one underneath the number seventeen yawns open, its retrieving door ripped off.

"Mama will be hysterical." Pavlik takes out the newspaper, unfolds it and walks up the stairs.

A piece of paper floats out. I pick it up. It's a lined page from a school notebook scrawled with large childish letters.

PAVEL BABOCH, KOSTYA PROBABLY FORGOT TO TELL YOU BECAUSE HIS FAGGOT FACE GOT SCRAGGED. YOU'RE NEXT, JEWISH HOMO. HAPPY COMING NEW YEAR, HAPPY NEW EXPERIENCES.

My insides freeze.

"Irina?" Pavlik returns for me.

I give him the note. *I saw them. I saw them leave, the ravens.*

"Is this for me?" He reads it and turns gray.

I snatch the paper out of his hands, crunch it into a ball, and fling it up the staircase. It lands by the garbage chute.

Fucking bastards! I hope you drown in dog piss, you rotten chickenshits, you—

"What did you do that for?"

I'm deaf from rage, shaking.

"Pavlusha?" Yulia's voice floats down from above.

"Pavlusha, is that you?" Her slippers shuffle down and she halts by the chute, an empty trash pail in her hand. "I was taking out the garbage and I thought I heard your voice."

From the fifth floor. Really?

She intercepts my gaze, spots the note and picks it up.

"No!" Pavlik rushes up the stairs.

"What's this?"

I cover my face. *What did I do, what did I do.*

"What does this mean?" Yulia's voice shakes.

"Mama, please, I can explain."

"Yulechka?" Anton shouts from above. "Are you all right? I'm coming down."

I steep in guilt. I hear them whisper, hear them mount the stairs. I trail behind them, unseeing and unfeeling.

As soon as the door is locked, Yulia explodes. "Read it!" She thrusts the note into Anton's hands.

"Mama, please, can we do this without hysterics? It's just a joke, someone played a prank on me, that's all." Pavlik smiles, but his eyes dance with mortal terror.

"Hysterics?" Yulia's mouth works. "Did you say, hysterics?"

"A death threat?" says Anton. "Jewish homo?"

Pavlik's face goes ashen.

My conscience torments me and I rush to the balcony, pull out the notebook and the pen from under the stool, and scribble.

IT'S SHAKALOV. HE HAS A PORTRAIT IN HIS OFFICE OF ONE OF THE RUSSIAN NATIONAL UNITY PEOPLE. HE MUST WORK FOR THEM. HE THINKS ALL OF SIM'S ACTORS ARE GAY AND HE HATES GAYS.

I run back and give it to Anton.

"Is this a joke?" he says quietly.

Yulia peers over his shoulder. "A jackal?"

"Can we talk about this tomorrow?" Pavlik's eyes widen.

He stares at me. "Irina is tired, I'm tired. My leg is acting up."

I lose all feeling in my body.

Anton hands me back the notepad.

IT'S THE JACKAL. IT HAS A HEAD IN ITS LAIR OF ONE OF THE RAVENS. IT MUST HUNT FOR THEM. IT THINKS ALL OF THE SEAL'S PUPS ARE PARROTS AND BUTTERFLIES AND IT HATES THEM.

I drop it.

CHAPTER FIFTEEN

FOX

It's the evening of the New Year. We stand on the seventh floor of the nine-story Brezhnevka and watch the brown vinyl door with the plastic number 62 over the spy-hole. Yulia is in her snakeskin coat, her gloved finger on the bell. It ding-dongs brightly. Anton coughs, champagne and mandarins pressed to his chest. Pavlik sets two heavy plastic bags onto the floor. They hold glass jars of Olivier salad, herring under fur coat, pickled mushrooms, and caviar.

I grip a carton with the Bird's Milk cake, my favorite. I grip it so hard that I'm afraid I'll crumple it. The moment we stepped out of the elevator I heard buzzing. Harsh, hostile buzzing coming from the apartment on the opposite end of the landing. I want to shut my ears to stop the noise, the texture of the hum, the rubbing of the wings and the mandibles and the hairy legs.

Horseflies, pissing themselves rotten.

I'd recognize this sound anywhere. My heart thrums hard. I'm bolted to the floor, afraid to move.

What if they open the door? What if—

The elevator jolts to life. Its mechanism revolves with a kind of an ominous whirr.

Yulia rings the bell again.

Someone croaks several floors below and enters the cabin.

A raven?

I glance at Pavlik.

He answers with his practiced theater smile. For the last three weeks to every note I have written about ravens he has given me this smile. Pleasant, gracious, empty.

And you tell me I'm in denial.

"She's probably in the bathroom," says Yulia, and presses the bell button. The echoes die and out floats an old woman's voice, muffled, irritated, and brittle.

"I'm coming! I'm coming! No need to rouse the whole house."

There's a labored patter of feet, the rasping and creaking of the locks, and there she stands, her arms akimbo. Seventy-something, petite, and rugose, gray hair hennaed flaming red and pulled into a tight bun. Sharp nose, sharp eyes.

A fox. Old and toothless, but a fox nonetheless.

"Mama, what took you so long?" says Yulia.

"We brought your favorite treats, Margarita Petrovna." Anton offers her the goods. "Champagne, mandarins, and there is the herring under fur coat in that bag. It took Yulechka all day to make it."

And I was just a fixture in the kitchen.

"Grandma! Happy coming New Year," says Pavlik.

She doesn't reply, jabs me with her eyes. "A bit too fat and a bit too short, but what can you do. I suppose it's too late now." She nods her chin at Pavlik. "At least she's got a good size bum, something for you to hold on to."

He flushes.

"Mama—"

"Don't you mama me, and don't just stand there. Come in. You're letting out all of my warm air."

The green from Yulia's face is gone in an instant.

I grin. *Margarita Petrovna, I like you.*

Yulia recovers quickly. "Well, we can't come in with you standing in the door, can we?"

The elevator arrives on our floor and I'm too terrified to look. I step over the threshold and hear the door behind me click shut. I prop my back on the wall to stop from falling.

Margarita's apartment is a one-room hole crammed with knick-knacks, blankets, shawls on the backs of chairs, photographs in dusty frames, and rugs. Rugs on every surface. Woven, knotted, tufted, crocheted from old cut-up pantyhose. In the middle of the room stands the celebratory table covered with an embroidered cloth, mixed china, glasses, and what looks like a big plate of jellied fish.

Pavlik takes the carton from my stiff hands and tramps after his parents into the kitchen. Margarita helps me out of my coat and nudges me to the table.

I sit on the chair next to the TV cabinet and a scraggly New Year's tree decked out in ornaments and silver tinsel. Behind the window, in the darkness, glow windows of other Brezhnevkas, the nightly Moscow landscape to light up with fireworks at midnight.

The clock on top of the TV shows it's after eight.

Margarita studies my belly.

Are you as blind as them?

"That's a big strong baby you got there." She pats me with a crooked hand. "Who would've thought, our Pavlushka was born tiny. This one has got to be taking after you. I hope it won't tear you when the time comes."

I shrug, uneasy.

"Yulia tells me you're an invalid. I say, nonsense. What invalid? You don't look like an invalid to me. Childbirth will make you talk, you'll see. You won't just talk, you'll be cursing my grandson like the lowest dog," she titters.

No, it's the boar I'll be cursing.

"Mama, you didn't have to!" Yulia walks in and wedges salad bowls between dishes on the table. "I told you not to cook, but you never listen. At your age, you have to think about your health."

"Yulia, shut your trap."

I hear Yulia's teeth clack. My lips stretch on their own accord and it takes an enormous effort to stop them.

"I'm fine," says Margarita. "I told you I'd cook. What's all this?" She jabs a shaky finger. "What did you bring this for? You think I can't afford to feed you on my own?" She stands up, shorter than her daughter.

Yulia shrinks.

"I'm not dead yet, thank God, so stop fussing around me. Better fuss around your future daughter-in-law."

"Sure, Mama. I'm only worried about your heart—"

"Leave my heart alone! It's fine. Worry about your own."

Yulia's lips are one hard line.

I positively glow.

"Margarita Petrovna, tea." Anton brings in an enameled kettle and teacups and Pavlik is on his heels with napkins and the Bird's Milk cake on a platter.

"Well? Why are you standing? What did I cook this for? Sit." She winks at me.

I hide a grin.

We eat dinner.

Everything tastes good and I'm ravenous and stuff my face.

Margarita insists on serving the food herself, like a proper hostess. She moves about with surprising agility, chats up Yulia and Anton about their jewelry shop, Pavlik about his acting, and gives me a tattered notebook and a dull pencil to participate in the conversation.

I can't write.

The buzz is back.

The buzz and the croaking and the commotion in the flat across the landing. It sounds like the raven and one of the horseflies are fighting. The raven raises its beak. The rest of the horseflies retreat. Then the door on the landing slams. There are male voices, drunken and irate, and the whine of the descending elevator.

"I think the raven wants to eat the horsefly," I scrawl, and elbow Pavlik.

"Just a second," he says without looking, in the middle of recounting his recent performance to Margarita.

I want to get out, to see for myself.

I hesitate.

What if I'm wrong? What if it's nothing?

Anton turns on the TV. The screen throws a blue glare at our faces. Midnight is half an hour away, then it's fireworks and the presidential address.

I wonder how drunk you'll be this time, dear president, proclaiming that no political crisis is happening in the country, and boasting fake patriotic pride. Sure, let's pretend. Let's watch the Little Blue Light, Russia's dumbest variety show, and envy rich pop stars and famous cosmonauts and heroes of social labor hung with medals that are worth a pile of crap. Please, I want to puke.

I strain to listen through the TV noise. It's suddenly quiet. I don't like it.

"—told you, it needs to be done properly," Margarita is saying. "Go see her mother and have a talk with her, for God's sake."

Whose mother?

"Of course, Margarita Petrovna, of course. We'll go in January, isn't that what we decided, Yulechka?" Anton downs a shot of vodka.

"Yes, that's right," Yulia says. "Right after—"

"Wait a second." Pavlik puts up a hand. "How is it that I know nothing about this?"

Never mind the mute girl. My pulse is loud in my ears and my throat is dry. In January, I'm going back to that shithole. That place with cats and dogs and mounds of dirty dishes in the filthy kitchen. Lenochka's jeering mouth and Sonya's cruel jokes and my disheveled mama, drunk and half-naked. Grandma with her hideous laugh. And Lyosha Kabansky.

Do I get to eat it when we visit?

Eaglet! I cradle my belly.

It swirls inside me, then it kicks me with something sharp, an elbow or a knee. I gasp, surprised. It hurts.

Do I? says the eaglet.

Yes. Yes, I promise.

"Does it give you a hard time, the little beastie?" says Margarita.

I shake my head.

"Do you know if it's a boy or girl?"

"No, Mama, we don't know yet. We're going to see my gynecologist for an examination, some tests, and an ultrasound," says Yulia. "First week of January." She pins me with her green eyes. "She's one of the best doctors in Moscow. Very sought after, very hard to see."

I stiffen.

"I'm coming with you," says Pavlik, and takes my hand under the table. I squeeze it.

"What for, Pavlusha?"

"What do you mean, what for? It's my baby."

I begin to sweat.

"I tell you, Pavlushka, that's no business for men. Leave it to the women, you already did your part," Margarita titters.

"Mama!"

"What? Mama what? I told you not to mama me. I say what I want to say in my own house, and I don't want to hear any different." She smacks the table. "At my age, I don't give a damn. You think he doesn't know how to make babies? Look at her. What, you think she's got a hernia, or what?"

Red creeps up Yulia's cheeks.

"One minute to midnight!" Anton reaches for the champagne bottle and removes the foil.

"Already?" says Yulia.

"Fifty seconds now." He props the bottle on his stomach and turns it back and forth. With a loud pop, the cork hits the ceiling. Fizzy froth spumes over his hand and he pours it into the glasses.

We all stand and count back the seconds.

"Ten, nine, eight..."

The TV screen shows the black-and-gold clock of the Spasskaya Tower.

"...Three. Two. One."

The golden hand strikes twelve. The chimes ring out.

"Happy New Year! Happy new luck!"

We clink our glasses and I drink. It's bubbly and sweet.

The face of the president appears, ruddy and raw, like that of a skinned bear.

"Dear citizens of Russia," he says, and that's when it happens.

The fireworks start.

And the killing.

CHAPTER SIXTEEN

RAT

I drop my glass. I can hear them. The raven croaks and repeatedly pecks on the horsefly. It bucks beneath it, buzzing. The sound is like that of hammering, something sharp on something soft. They fly around the apartment, bump into walls. I listen, greedy for more. The horsefly tangles itself in what must be some wires and jitters, unable to flee, and the raven strikes and strikes and—

"Irina, what's wrong? Are you afraid of the fireworks?"

I shake my head.

"Come on." Pavlik pulls me to the window where Yulia, Anton, and Margarita already stand, watching the sky burst with flashes of silver and red and blue.

I brush him off and whisk out of the room and into the

hallway, fumbling with unfamiliar locks. My head swims, my hands shake, and my fingers are clammy and slippery.

It's killing it, it's killing it.

I bang the door open. Biting cold hits my face, hot from champagne and the cozy warmth of Margarita's apartment. Hurried footfalls skid down the stairs several floors below.

The raven!

A woman of undeterminable age appears in the door across the landing. She could be twenty, or she could be forty. A shabby lurex dress is stretched over her bony frame. Her eyes roll up to their whites on her peaked little face. Her hands reach into her bleached hair, her mouth opens, and she screams.

I cover my ears.

She runs out of air, takes a shuddering breath, and screams again. The echo pogoes up and down the staircase.

A rat, high on some shit, I bet.

Calls drift out behind me.

"Irina!"

"What is happening over there?"

"Who is that screaming?"

I walk up to her.

She regards me with a milky, unseeing gaze and folds on my chest. I stagger under her weight, edge in. The apartment is dim and squalid. A narrow corridor with stripped-off wallpaper, in places showing bare concrete. A crooked woodworm-eaten wardrobe. Cardboard boxes filled with all kinds of junk stacked against the walls. Soiled rags strewn about, pots and shoes and empty liquor bottles.

The woman sobs into the hollow of my neck. Her face is wet and her breath stinks of bootleg, garlic, and cheap cigarettes.

"Roma," she wheezes. "My Roma..."

Roma. One second I'm cold all over; in another, boiling

fury overwhelms me. *Fucking uncle Roma.*

"Irina, what are you doing here?" Pavlik warily steps inside. "What is going on?"

Yulia seizes his arm. "Pavlusha, leave it. Get her away from this woman and this nasty place. Oh, the smell." She waves a hand in front of her face.

On the landing, doors open and feet sally out, voices asking for the source of the noise. Someone says that it must be Svetka's friends engaging in debauchery again and it's nothing to worry about. Someone suggests calling militia.

"Mama, please stop. Excuse me." Pavlik taps on Svetka's shoulder. "We heard you screaming. Can we help you somehow?"

The woman unglues from me, stares at him uncomprehendingly. Black trails of mascara run down her cheeks. Her thin chest seesaws and she points to the double doors ajar in the middle of the corridor, the paint on them chipped, the glass panels replaced with warped plywood. "Roma...my Roma..."

He's in that room. I'm flooded with so much emotion, I can't move.

Anton steps in. "Pavlusha, let's call the medics. They'll know what to do."

"Are you kidding? Do you know how long it will take them to get here? On New Year's? They're seeing boozy dreams by now."

"Papa is right. There is nothing we can do. She seems to be heavily intoxicated. Besides, it's none of our business."

Pavlik ogles her. "Really?"

"Let me in. Let me in!" Margarita elbows her way through.

Svetka suddenly grabs my shoulders, shakes me, and wails in my face. "It's Vadik! You hear me? Vadik. He stabbed him!

The little bastard stabbed my Roma!"

There is a collective intake of air.

I clasp her wrists and remove her hands from me, ecstatic, terrified. I want to see it with my own eyes.

"I'll kill you!" Svetka's eyes clear. She straightens. "I swear. Vadik, you hear me! You little bitch! I'm going to kill you!" She jostles people aside and staggers out onto the landing, and I hear her tumble down the stairs and fall with a sickening crunch and curse and scream.

Stomping feet follow her.

Bedbugs in pursuit of an injured rat.

I use the moment and rush through the double doors and freeze.

Hideous flesh-toned wallpaper is smeared with streaks of blood, as if someone was chased around the room and shoved against the walls and knifed and chased again. There is no furniture except a bed by the wall to the right with a tangle of soiled sheets and a couple overturned stools next to a broken plate, a hunk of bread, and strewn-around empty bottles of vodka and beer.

Zhigulevskoe. Mama's favorite.

On the left, in the far corner, lies a fallen New Year's tree decked out in the same silver tinsel, shiny shards of broken globs scattered all around it.

I step closer.

Behind the tree lies a man, stiff and unnaturally bent at the waist. His trousers are unbuckled and he wears nothing else. His stomach is a sieve, a bloody mess. Whoever killed him was mad and careless. One of his arms is flung over his face as if in protection. I need to make sure. I nudge his arm with the tip of my slipper and it thumps to the floor.

If I could scream, I would, but my vocal cords lock.

Nothing exists for me but his face.

Roma.

His eyes are watery blue, vacant, staring into nothing. His mouth is half-open, as if in wonder.

My teeth begin to chatter and I cross over into rage. I step into the pool of his blood; the soft soles of Margarita's slippers soak it in. I don't care.

You piece of shit.

I raise my foot and kick him in the groin.

You fucking rapist.

I buffet his stomach, his chest, his face. The slippers make disgusting squelching noises. His body jerks lifelessly. His eyes are glassy, indifferent. It infuriates me even more.

You pervert! You degenerate! You scum!

Kicking is not enough. I drop to my knees and fist him, methodically, like a machine. Blood splatters me. Spruce needles cling to my skin. I hear Pavlik call my name, sense hands on me, trying to pull me away. I wriggle out and punch more. Someone seizes me by the armpits and drags me off.

"Irina, stop it! Stop it!"

I try to grab on to something, anything, to get back, to do more damage. My hands are sticky. Tears wet my eyes. And the smell of Roma's blood is on me, in my hair and in my clothes and in my bones.

I'm not done, I just started!

My feet catch on some box, the slippers slide off. I'm hauled into the corridor and out of the apartment.

I hope your death was painful! I want to scream in Roma's face. *I hope you suffered! I wish I was there to see it. I wish I was the one who killed you!*

They drag me across the landing and into Margarita's flat. I fight and bite and scratch, but there are too many of them and

I grow weak and let them take me into the kitchen and prop me onto a chair, placing a wet towel on my forehead and shoving pills into my mouth. A hand gives me a glass of water and I drink it all.

My head throbs and I retch.

Someone helps me to the bathroom, helps me stick my head under cold water so that it runs over my face and hands.

I stand like this for a long time, watching the water turn pink from the washed off blood, and then I start laughing. I choke on the water, spit it out, hold on to my stomach and laugh and laugh and laugh.

Then I notice Pavlik.

He stares at me, his face as white as a sheet.

I catch my breath.

"You scared me to death." He hands me a towel. "Why did you do it?"

I smile. *I kicked the shit out of him. He's dead, Pavlik, dead!*

"Please, look at me." He lifts my chin. "This is bad, really bad. Mama and Papa think you've gone crazy."

My smile grows bigger. *I have. So what, I don't care. Let them think what they want.*

"I don't know what to tell them, Irina."

I falter. *What do you mean?*

"Honestly, I don't know anymore." He tugs at his hair. "Can you explain what is going on? You haven't been yourself lately, you know, you're always gone in your head, we hardly ever talk, and now this...I don't know what to think."

A kick in my diaphragm.

I bend.

You let a bit of the animal out, says the eaglet.

Did I?

Yes. But I'm still hungry.

You'll get the boar, I promise. Really soon.

I feel dizzy and sway, slumping on the edge of the bathtub. Pavlik holds me and I hide my face in the nook of his arm and he strokes my hair.

"I'm sorry, Irina, I'm really sorry. It came out wrong. I didn't mean it like this. I don't think you're crazy." He pauses. "I saw what you wrote."

I raise my face.

"The raven wants to kill the horsefly." He studies me. "Was that...the horsefly? One of the guys who—"

I nod.

"How did you know?"

I tap on my ear.

"You heard it?"

I nod again and hide my face.

"But how?"

I shrug.

"But that's impossible. I was in the same room with you and I didn't hear anything."

I mime the fly and the raven chasing it along the edge of the sink, knock with a fingernail on the enamel to make a hammering noise.

Pavlik looks at me, a strange light in his eyes, a mix of fear and admiration. "I can't believe it. You heard them through all that noise? The TV and the fireworks..."

We stay silent for a moment.

"You know, now that I think about it, if I were in your place, I would've done the same thing. I'm actually jealous."

There is a knock on the door.

"Can I come in?"

Yulia orders Pavlik out and throws me one of Margarita's robes to change into. It's reddish-brown and smells of mothballs.

I strip, step into the tub, wash the blood off my feet, and then climb out, don the robe, and tie it with the belt.

I look at myself in the mirror, feeling victorious, and get out of the bathroom.

It's very quiet. The door into the room is closed. Anton surfaces from the kitchen and waves me to the wardrobe.

"Get dressed." His words are sharp.

My heart falls. I step into my boots, fling on the coat, and before I know it, he hooks his arm into mine and escorts me out of the apartment.

The door across the hall is closed and the landing is deserted.

We ride down the elevator in silence, get out of the building, and cross the street to Anton's Lada parked head-in at the opposite curb.

It's dawn. The sky is tinged with pink. Pigeons peck at the frozen ground in search of food. There is no sign of militia.

They're probably drunk.

Fresh snow crimps under my boots.

Anton opens the passenger door. "Quick."

I squeeze in and gasp. The seat is freezing.

It takes Anton a couple of tries to get the engine going. It rattles as it idles. He turns on the fan to full power and steps out. I hear him open the trunk and slam it shut. He shaves the frost off the windows with a scraper and sweeps the snow off the roof with a brush. I rub my arms, watching him work.

He gets in, wipes the windshield with a dingy towel, cleans his glasses on a kerchief, puts them on, and backs out.

And I see them.

A black Boomer, clean and polished, rolls slowly past us. For a moment our windows are level. The tinted glass slides down. Two men in black caps and black coats look out at me

with dull, expressionless eyes.
    I grip the seat.
    The ravens.

CHAPTER SEVENTEEN

OWL

Hands shake me. I sleepwalk up the stairs and crawl into bed and drop into a dreamless void. It seems like no time has passed when my burning bladder wakes me. The clock on Pavlik's desk shows five minutes after eight. Is it eight in the evening? No, it's morning. The darkness behind the window is too thin and the glowing orbs of the streetlights are dimming. Snow falls softly. *I have slept all day and all night.* I step into slippers and rub my face. The teakettle whistles faintly, chokes, and peters out.

I go to the toilet, then head for the kitchen.

Anton and Yulia drink tea. They look at me with irritation, as if I'm late and they've been waiting for me for hours.

I halt, puzzled. *Where is Pavlik?*

"Pavlik is with Margarita Petrovna, Irina. Please, sit down," says Yulia. "We're going to have a little talk."

My spine turns to ice.

The notebook I've been writing in sits next to Anton's teacup. He picks it up and smacks it down in front of me. Its fake leather cover meets the oilcloth with a gluey sticky noise. "Explain." He holds out a pen.

I take it, terrified, thinking that they have read my answers to Pavlik's questions and know who the father of the baby is, but then I remember that to them it would've looked like nonsense.

"Go ahead." Droplets of sweat prickle Anton's forehead. He takes his glasses off, polishes them with the hem of his shirt, and props them back on.

Did you understand what I meant?

"You're a jokester, aren't you?"

No, you didn't. I exhale in relief.

He shakes his head in dismay. "Start from the very beginning, and none of this drivel about any fish or jackals or any animals at all. Is that clear?" He slaps the table with the flat of his palm.

I flinch.

"I want you to explain to me why you stopped talking when you were two—"

So you called them.

"—what was the exact cause, and if there are any genetic deviations in your family, any terminal diseases, health problems, that sort of thing. Write everything you know." He measures me with a shrewd look.

I glare. *Is this an interrogation? Did you send Pavlik off so that you two could harass me without him?*

"Here is what I think. I think you're fooling us. I think you're pulling our noses. Either that, or you are, indeed, a bit soft upstairs." He knocks on his head. "That's what I think.

Wouldn't you agree, Yulechka?"

"Absolutely." Yulia stings me with an acid stare.

I seethe. *This automatic assumption that if you're mute, you're an imbecile, is really getting on my nerves. I thought you were educated people.*

Anton sips his tea. "Irina, if you are a smart girl, you will understand where we're coming from. We're simply trying to rule out any pathologies. You must agree that your behavior, the unexplainable things you have done in the two months that we've known you, have planted certain doubts in our minds as to the state of your mental health. Whatever it is, it doesn't concern you alone anymore, it concerns Pavlusha's child, our grandchild. Right, Yulechka?"

"Right."

I grip the pen so hard I think it will break. *You must be what, in your fifties? Well-read, I assume. Yet you believe that I'm crazy because I'm mute, I refer to people as animals, and I kicked a dead man. More, you believe my child will be predisposed to the same, as you call them, pathologies. Just because I did what I did doesn't mean I'm nuts and it doesn't mean that my child will be crazy, either. I see you know jack-shit about life, which at your age is, frankly, quite amusing.*

"Well?" says Anton.

Yulia crosses her arms.

Words crowd behind my teeth, wanting to break out. *Your logic points me to either stagnant thinking or complete ignorance. Have you noticed that your son is gay? No. You choose to be blind. And when you can't ignore it anymore, you will cast him aside because he doesn't fit your image of the perfect son. Because he has a pathology.*

I write one word. "No."

Anton cradles his temples. "How am I to understand that?"

I smile. *Guess.*

He throws a worried look at Yulia.

She has a smug look on her face.

"This is outrageous." His round eyes round even more. "We're wasting our time. Can't you see she's playing us?" He rises, catches on the edge of the table. Spoons clink and the tea slopes over.

Yulia picks a towel from the hook by the sink and mops it up. "If you'd only listen to me."

"But, Yulechka, if it's not genetic, how else can you explain it?"

"I told you, we need to talk to her mother."

Good luck catching her sober. I marvel at my calm. My future is at stake, yet I don't panic.

Anton draws aside the curtain and watches the snow.

I follow his gaze, searching for winged shapes. *How much longer before you strike? How much longer?*

Yulia spoons sugar into her cup and swills it. "Irina, I'll be straightforward with you, all right? We're taking you into our family but we hardly know you. It's a big and scary step for us. We're doing it for Pavlusha. He seems to be very much in love with you."

My heart clenches. *If you only knew.*

"Personally, I have my reservations. You'll understand"— she narrows her eyes to slits—"when you become a mother."

Anton turns away from the window. "Look, the sooner you do it, the sooner we can move on to discussing pleasant things. The wedding, the restaurant, your dress, your jewelry."

Something in my face causes them to exchange a satisfied glance.

I grit my teeth. *You know who you are, Irina Myshko? You're a bribable doormat.* But I can't help it. I imagine a white gown, a bridal veil, and kissing. My face burns. Kissing! He'd have to kiss me in front of everybody. Then I remember about the gynecologist. Never mind. As soon as they find out, it's back to Lyosha Kabansky. Might as well play along for as long as I can.

I pick up the pen and write.

I write about my school, my home, and every visit to the doctor I can remember. About mama, grandma, Sonya, and Lenochka. Our cats, our dogs. The stories I liked to invent in my head since I was little, pretending that different people were different animals. And I write about Lyosha. I don't mention anything bad, only good things. At the end, I tell them I had a fight with mama and that's why I ran away. Then I add one more line.

"When I was two, I fell out of my crib, bit my tongue, and stopped talking."

"Is that really what happened?" Anton peers at me through his glasses. He seems relieved.

I nod.

"That's all? You just fell out of the crib and bit your tongue?"

I shrug.

"Why did you have to climb, you silly girl?" He chuckles.

I squeeze the pen.

"We'll ask her mother for more details, all right?" says Yulia sweetly. I sense controlled irritation. "I need your phone number, please."

I write it down.

Yulia makes to take the notebook from me.

Anton stops her. "Hold on, hold on. One more thing, if I may. Irina, tell us. What made you hit that unfortunate young man?"

"He hurt me," I write.

"You knew him?"

"Hurt you how?" says Yulia.

Ever had horseflies bite your cunt?

I slam the pen down and race out of the kitchen and into Pavlik's room. I fall onto his bed and bury my head under the pillow, sobbing into the sheets until I'm barren.

Yulia's voice comes through the door. "Irina?"

I sit up. I must have dozed off.

"Get dressed, we're leaving."

Right now?

I brush off my clothes, fix the bed, and walk out.

Yulia sits on the sofa, dialing the phone number from my notebook. She looks up at me with her green eyes. "Hello?"

"Who is this?"

The voice is so loud that I can hear it.

Yulia winces, looks at the receiver, puts it back to her ear at a distance. "Yes. This is Yulia Davydovna—"

"Who?" yells the voice. "Kesha, get off me, you dumb bitch. Say again?" There is muffled barking.

Hey, Grandma, it's so nice to hear you.

"One more time, my name is Baboch, Yulia Davydovna. I have your Irina, Irina Myshko. She's been living with us for a couple months now."

"Who? Irkadura? Where?"

Yulia recoils at my nickname and gives me a questioning look. "Yes, she is sitting right here, in front of me."

"Marina, it's your Irka! Quick!"

There is a short pause, then mama's voice shouts. "Hello? Hello? Who is this? Hello?"

"Yes?"

"Where is my daughter?"

Yulia holds the receiver away from her face, staring at it with aversion. The corners of her lips turn down. She gives me another questioning look.

I don't move.

"Where is my daughter? Give me back my daughter! Who are you? I'm asking, who are you, huh? What a nightmare! I went through such a nightmare! I thought she got shot by the White House! Can you hear me? Hello? Hello?"

Get a grip, Mama. Yet I like it. I revel in her reaction. It seems as though she actually cares.

Yulia consults the notebook. "Marina Viktorovna—"

"What?"

"I said, Marina Viktorovna!"

"Yes, I'm listening."

"Please, calm down. Your daughter is fine." Yulia waves me off.

My legs are suddenly full of water. I tread to the hallway and slowly pull on my boots, put on my coat, button it up with unbending fingers, sit down on the little stool by the door, and wait.

What if I do have a pathology? What if my mother is mentally ill and it's genetic and I have it too? Are there tests for this? Can they tell?

In a few minutes, Yulia is done with the call. She zips up her leather boots, puts on her fur coat and hat, and slings her snakeskin purse over the shoulder. "Ready?"

I don't have the strength to nod.

An hour later we exit from the Nogin's Square station into the old Moscow center. The wind nips my nose and the gray sky sits low on the roofs of the low buildings with scuffed stuccoed facades. Trucks rumble through the street. Hunched, bundled from head to toe, figures scurry by.

I stuff my mittened hands into my pockets and hurry after Yulia along the pathway stomped in the snow by hundreds of feet. I watch for signs of anything living on the sloped roofs and poles and wires. I see nothing and soon give up.

This is your walk to your execution, Irina Myshko.

We pass an old church, a bakery with its bread smell, a bank, and a couple of shoe stores, then cross the street and enter a low-arched passageway that leads into a web of inner courtyards.

I walk behind Yulia, my head down, my eyes on the road.

She talks non-stop, about how she took precious time out of her day to take me to her gynecologist, how Karina Semyonovna is very hard to get an appointment with, how it's a privilege that she agreed to see me at all, how it was only because she's an old friend of Yulia's and how Yulia is doing me a favor, how I should be thankful to her and how—

I sense movement behind us, and look back.

A black Boomer crawls through the narrow alleyway framed by waist-high walls of dirty snow on either side.

"Watch out!" Yulia yanks me out of the way.

I press flat against the snowbank.

The car whispers by. The tinted passenger window rolls down and a man measures me with disinterested eyes. A black cap sits tightly around his shaved head.

I grope behind me for purchase.

I know what you want. You want to free Mother Russia from a homo Jew, his whore, and their bastard.

A raven croaks in the distance.

My heart does a summersault.

Yulia motions after the car. "What polite young men."

I stare at her.

"Didn't honk, didn't berate us. They slowed down and waited for us to notice them. Now that is a sign of education and wealth." She lowers her voice. "You need to learn how to stand on your own two feet, Irina."

Is this a ploy to make me bring money home so that I won't sit on your son's neck, or do you miraculously care all of a sudden?

"You need to learn how to be independent." Warm breath escapes Yulia's painted lips. "You can't rely on your husband, no matter how much you love him and no matter how much he loves you. Love has nothing to do with it. If something happened to Anton, I'd be able to survive on my own. Would you?"

I have my fat ass to fall on.

"No, you wouldn't. You have nothing, Irina, not even a college degree. And you're mute. How do you plan to live? On what money? You either have to go to college and get a degree or get Simeon Ignatievich to hire you. He seems to have a thing for you. Use it. To survive in this life, a woman has to use everything she has. You have a good face and a good figure. You just need to lose weight once the baby is born, that's all."

I stop breathing. *Use Sim? I'll need to grow a dick for that.*

A car honks and, once again, we press into the snowbank to let it through.

"I know what you think. You think that I don't like you."

I stand still.

"You're wrong. I'm simply cautious, like any mother should be. I'm sure you'd do the same for your child." Wind moves the fur on her hat. She steps closer. "Tell me the truth. Is it Pavlusha's?"

For a split second I'm caught off-guard, then I nod.

"Are you sure?"

I nod vigorously several times.

"Good. I wanted to see it in your eyes. Come on, we're late." She grabs my hand.

It's the first time she touched me.

I trot behind her, feeling guilty.

CHAPTER EIGHTEEN

SALAMANDER

We arrive at a two-story clay brick building wedged between an apartment block and a squalid government institution. A few empty prams are parked by the entrance. A lone father in a tattered coat and a beanie jumps from foot to foot and smokes a cigarette. People bustle in and out. Pregnant women, women with babes in their arms, old women in kerchiefs, harried mothers with little children in tow. The signboard above the door says City Polyclinic Number 7, Women's Consultation.

"Hurry, hurry!" Yulia pulls on my hand.

Inside, it's warm and stuffy like in a banya. The lobby is packed with bodies, sitting, standing, waiting. They form some kind of a line but it's impossible to tell the order or who is first and who is last. Yulia jostles through to the glass window that has REGISTRATION stamped on it in half-erased letters. The faces of those close to it watch her with mounting hostility.

A teenage girl—so large her coat won't button all the way—takes a medical record booklet from the pass-through slot and leaves. Immediately, a frail and sullen mother with a newborn in her arms, swaddled in a blanket and tied with a bow, leans in to speak. Before she can say a word, Yulia shoulders her out of the way.

"Good afternoon, we're here to see Karina Semyonovna."

The mother stares. "Where the hell are you going? It's not your turn!" Her baby begins to cry.

"Surname," asks the nurse in the booth. She's squat and waistless, her face round, red, and indifferent.

Like a boiled crayfish.

"Myshko," says Yulia.

"What's the matter, are you deaf, or what? Didn't you hear me? Get out of the way!"

Yulia shrugs her off.

The nurse slips the record booklet through the slot. "Second floor, room thirty-four."

Indignant voices are all around us.

"There is a line here!"

"You must take your place in the queue!"

"Some women have no shame!"

"Why did you serve her out of turn? I've been waiting for a whole hour and she barges in right in front of me like she owns the place. I'm going to complain!" The upset mother shakes her baby so hard its cries escalate to wails. Other babies join.

"Quiet!" says the nurse. "You're disturbing our work."

Yulia doesn't say anything, doesn't react at all. She forces her way through the crowd, tugging me after her to the end of the lobby and up the stairs to the second floor.

I stumble on the last stair.

The air is heavy with the smell of medicine and chlorine. My boot soles squeak on the linoleum floor. We rush along the hallway, passing doors and benches occupied by women in various stages of ripeness. Silent, stupefied from the long wait. Some knit, some scan magazines, others stare into nothing or nap.

Cows, bloated cows. Soon, I'll look the same.

Yulia undresses as she goes, motions me to do the same. I pull off my coat on the run, stuffing the knit hat and mittens in the sleeve. The door before the last opens and out glides a doctor in a white starched coat. She is short and slim and her skin is bronzed and oily. Broad flat nose, slanted eyes, dark hair plaited into a braid. She must be in her forties, but she looks much younger.

A toxic salamander, perfect viper friend.

She sees us. "Finally."

"Karina!" Yulia pants from running. "We were just—"

"I started to think you wouldn't show."

Several women are sitting on the benches by the door. Some have dozed off, the rest glare at us. One of them rises.

"Excuse me, Karina Semyonovna. I'm next."

"No. This woman said I am." Her neighbor points to one of the slumped figures.

"I don't know what she told you, and it's none of my business. I only know that I'm next and that's that."

"What are you saying?"

"What am I saying? I've been waiting for two hours—"

"And I haven't? I took my place in the queue like all of us did, didn't I? Girls, tell her."

"That's right, doctor. Why does she get to skip ahead?"

They look at me as if they want to kill me.

Karina doesn't say a word; she ushers us in and shuts the door.

The room is small and shabby. A writing desk, a cot, a couple of stools, a gynecological chair, a dying plant in a pot by the window, gray from dust.

"Karina, this is for you." Yulia digs in her purse and produces a box of chocolates and a small bottle of liquor.

"What's it for? I don't need it. Put it away. Put it away!" Karina lazily moves the bribe aside.

"No, please. I insist."

I breathe deeply to calm down and to stop the jittering. The only things I see are the gynecological chair and a tray of instruments next to it. *How much time do I have, before the lab returns the results? A week? Two weeks? A few days?*

The goods tucked into her desk, Karina asks me to undress.

I take my time getting out of my pants and panties and socks. My legs are numb. I climb up and plop onto the oilcloth seat and recline, wincing as I place my feet into the metal holders. They're freezing.

This is it.

Karina snaps on gloves, palpates my belly, and unceremoniously feels me out. "I'd say, five months? Five and a half, more like it."

Yulia appears to be doing a mental calculation. She frowns.

I squeeze the edges of the seat. *Was Pavlik even in Moscow in August?*

"Are you sure?"

Karina yanks her hand out. "Would you like to check yourself?"

"No, no. I believe you. It's just that—"

"Why didn't you come to see me earlier?"

"Oh, we were busy." Yulia smiles. "Karina, those tests we

151

talked about—"

"To determine paternity?"

My heart stills.

"Well, yes, that too, but I'm more worried about any pathological conditions. I want to make sure—"

"She really doesn't talk, does she? That's so strange." Karina studies me with her slanted eyes. "Are you afraid the baby might have a speech defect?"

There's an angry knock on the door.

Karina marches over and jerks it open. "You get in when you get in! I don't have ten arms! Now, if you stop interrupting me, you get in faster."

"But Karina Semyonovna, I've been waiting for two hours already. My daughter is sick, she's alone at home and she's only—"

The doctor slams the door in the woman's face.

"They think I'm their slave. I get paid meager kopecks to deal with this rubbish, every day, from eight to six. The stories they tell, you wouldn't believe. And now I forgot what I was going to do." She slaps her thighs.

"Tests," says Yulia. "And an ultrasound."

An ultrasound. How could I forget! I feel faint.

Eaglet.

Silence.

Eaglet?

Nothing.

Eaglet, I think I know who you are.

"I'll take her blood and urine today, but for the paternity one, I'll need DNA samples from both the parents and the child, so we'll have to do that one after her labor. It's expensive." Her eyes glint greedily.

"Oh," says Yulia. "How much?"

They discuss the price.

I tune out, warm with relief. I have four months, four whole months to figure things out.

Do you? asks the eaglet.

What? Eaglet!

You said you know who I am.

Yes, I do.

Who am I?

You're a boy.

A short pause. *How do you know?*

There is something about the way you talk, the way you never doubt things. You give me certainty, you fill me with a desire to destroy. It's very masculine. It makes me want to hurt the ones who have caused me pain.

The eaglet kicks me in the diaphragm. *Then hurry up and do it, because I'm hungry.*

I know. Soon.

Do I get it whole?

Yes, all yours, from lungs to liver, except its dick. The dick is mine. Something for me to hold on to, while I gut it.

Okay.

Eaglet?

Yes?

I'm asked to go to the toilet and to piss in the cup. A nurse pokes my fingers, my veins, and drains my blood.

Eaglet?

What is it?

I get dressed and walk to another room and lie down on the cot. There is a desk and a monitor on top of it and the same jelly gets squirted on my stomach by a different nurse. Yulia and Karina stand by my side, looking.

The grainy image flickers. There are the white lines

forming the triangular slice, only there is no black oval hole this time. This time, there is an outline of a fully formed baby.

Eaglet?

I'm here.

Eaglet!

I'm here!

The head turns toward me and the arm waves and I can't see it clearly because it's blurry. My eyes are wet.

"It's a boy," says the nurse.

Eaglet.

Mama.

I float back to the metro. I'm weightless. Every passerby seems to smile at me and I smile back. The sky is soft with snow clouds and the buildings are worn in that warm, inviting way. Pigeons peck at a discarded loaf of bread on the curb and the snow creaks underfoot, clean and white. I grab a handful and pop it in my mouth; it tastes sweet.

We enter the underpass to the Nogin's Square station and Yulia stops by a produce kiosk and a flower stall and gives me the bags to carry. Then she makes several calls from the pay phone by the ticketing booth. Commuters straggle by, slow and sleepy, as if in hibernation.

I watch them.

I will do it, eaglet. For you. I will learn how to talk.

We get back at dusk.

Pavlik and Anton rise from the sofa as one.

"Who is it?"

"It's a boy," says Yulia. She sounds pleased.

"A boy!" Anton rubs his hands. "That's great news. Congratulations." He pats Pavlik on the back.

Pavlik takes the bags from my hands, puts them on the floor, and helps me out of the coat. "A son." He searches my eyes, steals a glance back.

I shake my head slightly and flip up a thumb.

Don't worry, nobody knows.

He sighs in relief. "I'm sorry I couldn't make it. I had to stay with grandmother a little longer."

"How is she, by the way?" Yulia says from the parlor.

"Good. Never better. Frankly, I don't understand why you had me stay with her in the first place."

"Really?"

He closes his eyes for a second. "What should we call him?"

I shrug.

He suddenly lifts my face and whispers in my ear. "I know it sounds strange, but I'm happy. Are you happy?"

I pitch and hide my face in the folds of his shirt.

He holds me carefully, like a bowl of water that's about to spill, and I am.

I am.

CHAPTER NINETEEN

LOUSE

It's an hour from sunset on the next day. The sky is indigo, faint with stars. Mothers with prams stroll around the yard, children fight over a piece of cardboard by the ice slide. Voices and dog barks and glowing windows. Behind them, the warmth of cabbage soup, bone marrow spread on dark bread, television, and vodka. I hiccup, full of hastily swallowed cutlet and a glass of yoghurt, and climb into the car. Everyone is already seated.

The evening traffic is stop and go. Anton expresses his annoyance. Nonchalant, Yulia does her makeup.

Pavlik is gloomy and withdrawn.

I want to cheer him up, so I open the notebook. "We have four months. Four whole months."

He throws a frightened glance at his parents and shakes his

head and takes the pen from me and strikes out the words.

I snatch the pen back. "You can refuse to give your DNA sample."

"Don't," he says under his breath.

I move my hand out of his reach. "What will they do? Force you?"

He sucks in air.

We stop at the red light. Anton launches into a spiel on the terrible condition of traffic in Moscow. Yulia placates him.

"After a while they'll forget, and we can—" I follow Pavlik's gaze.

He stares at a car parked by the curb. KILL A FAG, SAVE THE PLANET is scrawled on its snow-covered window.

"It's the ravens. They followed me yesterday."

Pavlik studies what I've written. "What?"

"When your mother took me to see the gynecologist, a black Boomer trailed me. I'm certain it was those Nazi people. Have you gotten any more threats?"

He averts his eyes. His fingers are laced, trembling.

"You need to tell Sim. He'll think of something. It can't go on like this forever, they will strike, you know." I pause and add, "I think you need to tell your parents that you're—"

His eyes flash. He wrests the notepad from my hand, tears off the page, crumples it, winds down the window and throws it out. Cold wind drifts in, blares, squealing tires, a street vendor's cry, "Chiburekki! Hot Chiburekki!"

Yulia drops her lipstick. "Pavlusha! Why did you open the window? Close it. It's freezing."

"With pleasure, Mama."

I sense that he is on edge and it puts me on edge, too. That, and the faint squall of birds coming from somewhere afar. I peer into the darkness and see streetlights, storefronts, nothing.

Where are you hiding?

We crawl to a stop at a huge intersection. It starts to snow.

"This is outrageous! Simply outrageous!" Anton slaps his knees. "Where are all the snowblowers? That's what I'd like to know."

"On strike, of course," says Yulia knowingly. "The less they work, the more they can drink."

"We won't make it by five, Yulechka. Not at this pace. I hate being late, you know that."

"Calm down. We'll get there when we get there."

I hear a croak so closely, it startles me. *Come out. I know you're here. That's enough of playing hide-and-seek.*

The light changes to green.

We take off in the midst of confusion. All lanes of the avenue are congested with cars and buses and trucks and heavily falling snow. Anton spins the wheel and wedges a little to the right only to be honked at and forced back.

A block ahead glows the big red letter M of the metro sign. Swarms of pedestrians press on either side of the road, waiting for the opportunity to cross.

I hear a new noise and my heart cramps. I recognize it. The bleating of a goat. It's accompanied by harsh bird cries coming from high above. They coil and loop, and with sudden clarity, I see what's coming. This time, it's not the vultures looking to feed on roadkill. It's the ravens, looking to kill.

There will be a death.

It's a signal for me, as if they're saying, *watch what happens to those who are not of pure Russian blood.*

The crosswalk is some thirty meters away. The flow of the cars ebbs and thins and, in minutes, traffic disperses and we begin to move faster.

I squint at the mass of bodies on the right sidewalk. It's

dark and I can barely make out faces from this distance; then I see her. The old hag in a tattered coat probing ahead of her with a cane.

The goat. I nudge Pavlik.

He looks at me, irritated. "What?"

I point.

"What is it?"

The goat that hit Kostya's car.

I grope for the notebook, but can't find it. We're almost level with her now, picking up speed.

She'll get hit!

It happens in seconds.

The light turns red.

Anton slams on the breaks and the Lada rolls over the white stripes of the crosswalk.

The hag hikes up her coat, hobbles over the curb, and staggers into the street, her cane thrust upward. She is the first, the rest of the pedestrians wisely remain standing, waiting for all of the vehicles to make a complete stop. A pair of headlights splash her. Two steps away from our Lada, she halts and turns to look, her mouth agape. I glimpse her face, wrinkled and startled. Shreds of greasy hair escape her headscarf. She hasn't realized yet what's about to happen and probably never would.

I hasten to wind down the window. My fingers slip off the handle. I wave, frantic with panic. *Get back to the curb! Now!*

It's futile.

A black car with tinted windows slams into her at full speed. Her body, a carcass of bones wrapped in a goat's hide, flies up, bumps the windshield once, cracks it, bounces upward, rolls along the roof, hits the trunk, turns once more, and drops onto the road.

"Oh God." Pavlik covers his mouth. "Oh God."

"She got hit!" Yulia is hysterical.

"Who got hit?" Anton leans over to look.

There is a rush of onlookers. Drivers step out of their cars. Those who are behind and can't see what's happening lay on their horns. Chaos ensues.

I'm immobile, staring ahead, watching the red lights of the Boomer. They flash and vanish in a side alley, and I hear them crack up, cackling and raving, drunk.

You damn chickenshits.

"Did you...see that coming?"

I rudely push Pavlik away, mad at him. Mad at everything and everyone.

Anton gets back in. Yulia looks at him questioningly. He spreads his arms and shrugs.

Nobody talks for the rest of the ride.

It's fully dark now. I recognize the dingy streets I grew up on and the massive block looming in the night. The nine-story Brezhnevka. My stomach churns. How long has it been? Since September. I glance up at the last floor, out of habit. Same windows, same glaring light from the naked forty-watt bulb in the kitchen.

I close my eyes.

You promised, says the eaglet.

I know.

You promised to feed me. Don't forget—

I won't. I won't.

Anton parks at the curb across the entranceway. I get out last. Every movement takes time, every step.

In the ring of light on the bench by the front door sits an old woman in felt boots with rubber overshoes, a mangy coat, and a fur hat. She struggles to get up.

Prasha, you louse, what are you freezing out here for?

I cross my arms to hide my belly, and then abandon the effort. If Prasha is here, that means the entire building already knows.

"Irka!" White puffs escape her mouth. "I just knew it! It's the angels that have brought you back. I put up a candle for you every time I went to church. Yes, I did." She hobbles up to Pavlik, her overshoes crunching in the snow. "Is this the groom then? Come here, let the old Prasha see."

He looks at me, puzzled.

Neighbor. I mime it. *Prasha is our neighbor. She used to take care of me when I was little.*

He doesn't get it.

"What are you looking at her for? She is mute, don't you know that by now? No good looking at her." Prasha offers him a mittened hand. "Praskovya Aleksandrovna is my name. I'm their neighbor across the landing."

"Pavel Baboch," says Pavlik, hesitant. "Nice to meet you."

"I've lived here for thirty-five years now, since it was built. Valentina and I used to work at the same hospital and we both got apartments here."

"Valentina?" Yulia frowns. "Is that—"

"Irka's grandmother. Didn't she write it all out for you? She's fond of writing, that one. Yes, she is."

Anton and Yulia exchange a glance.

"What a fine boy you got for yourself then." Prasha chews on her toothless mouth. "Good catch, Irka. Atta girl!" She pats on Pavlik's cheek. He is so surprised, he lets her.

"What coal eyes you've got. What coal eyes! What wouldn't I give to be young again, I'd fetch you for myself. Yes, I would." She wobbles up to me and claps on my belly. "What's that you got there then? A boy or a girl?"

"How about we come inside?" says Yulia.

I throw her a grateful glance.

"Yes, yes. What am I doing, holding you here. They've been waiting and waiting. I started to think I'd freeze to the bench!" She pulls the door open.

I step into the familiar smell: piss, rot, sour soup, and rancid garbage.

Home. I used to call this home.

It's nostalgic and unsettling, sweet and disgusting. I want to jump out of my skin and to spring without turning, but I can't. I have promised the eaglet.

I force myself up the steps.

Prasha talks nonstop. "I knew Irka since she was born. She used to be so small and so skinny, and look at her now. Look how she rounded out. Atta girl. She is like a daughter to me."

I'm like a daughter to no one.

Prasha presses the elevator button, it glowers red.

Several floors above the cabin begins laboring down.

"Valentina went to work at the crack of dawn every morning." Prasha's words are punctured with saliva. "She would leave Irka with me for the whole day. She's a nurse, Valentina, an honest woman. God forbid anyone to have a child like her Marinka. That's one worthless dura, her Marinka. She shouldn't have been allowed to have children, they should have fixed her in that clinic she went to. Valentina would put here there every spring and every fall. A whore, that's what she is. Squeezed Irka out and phew! Vanished. Men, men, only men on her mind. She brought home one mongrel after another. Poor Valentina. Scum, all of them. Alcoholics." Prasha hawks up a gob of saliva and spits. It plops onto the floor with a smack.

There is a silence and the whiz of machinery.

Pavlik raises a brow.

Anton and Yulia study Prasha with obvious dislike.

Wait until you see my family. Prasha is nothing.

The cabin thumps to a stop and yawns open.

After living in a building without an elevator, I peek inside with distrust. Same grimy linoleum floor, same spray-painted symbol of SPARTAK CHAMPION next to the panel with worn buttons, same stink.

Prasha stomps in first, I'm last. There's barely room for five people. I push the button numbered nine. The sliding doors roll shut and the elevator jerks upward.

And Prasha talks and talks and talks. She gives them my entire life history. How I was born weak and small, how I was often sick, and how I wet the bed till the fifth grade. How mama beat me for it. How our dogs and cats pissed through the floor and how the neighbors below, a respectable couple, complained, because the urine corrupted their ceiling. How Sonya hooked up with a new Russian millionaire and got ditched after he found out that she had a daughter. How Marina and Lyosha—

The doors mercifully open.

I stagger out, gulping for air.

The door to my right stares in my face. The left bottom corner is chewed off by the animals, its plastic numbers above the spy-hole are burned, and the metal handle is polished with wear.

Prasha shoves me aside and rings the bell.

At first, an uncertain bark, then a volley of them.

"Valentina, open up! It's Prasha!" She pounds on the door.

"Praskovya Aleksandrovna," says Yulia sweetly, "thank you very much for your help."

"Yes, thank you," says Anton. "You were very helpful. Good night."

"Please excuse us, Praskovya Aleksandrovna," says Pavlik, "we're just—"

"Yes, yes. I'll go." Prasha is crestfallen. She pats my cheek. "You're a smart girl, Irka, I always knew that. You marry this boy and get out of here. I'll keep putting up candles, for the angels to watch over you." She smooches me with her dry lips and retreats across the landing, fumbling with her keys.

There are no angels, Prasha, only ravens.

I turn around and face the door.

It flies open.

CHAPTER TWENTY

COCKROACH

I cover my nose. From the doorway comes that reek I detest. It strikes me like a solid physical being. Old sweat, animal stink. Moldy, unwashed linens. Alcohol fumes. Badly cooked food with too much fat and too much salt. The vapor permeates my clothes. I used to smell like that—my hair, my skin. I used to not notice it. It infiltrated me to the bones. My eyes water. I blink and I see them.

They're all standing there, waiting. Mama, Sonya, Lenochka, grandma. And Lyosha Kabansky. Kesha and Kasha yelp. Their floppy ears and fawn hides jitter from excitement. They wag their tails and jump at me and I give them my palms to lick and—

The beasts look at the mouse. The catfish, the two herrings, the cockroach, and the boar. It's huge and hairy and—

I take a shuddering breath.

Mama flings herself on me. "Daughter! My sweet daughter!"

I reel under her weight, her clammy skin and flabby flesh. This affection she always displays in front of strangers, an exaggerated attachment diametrically opposite to the hatred she gives me one on one. Her hangover washes over my face.

Kesha and Kasha whimper and scratch at my legs.

"Get off her! Dumb dogs." Mama kicks them.

They squeal, tuck their tails, and run off.

She strokes my hair. "Irka, my Irka. I thought you died. What's the matter with you, huh? Don't you want to kiss me?"

Would you want to kiss a catfish?

"Why? Why did you leave me like that? Have you no heart? Don't you love your mama? You should've told them to call us earlier. I've gone all gray worried about you." She lets go and rakes her greasy hair out of her face and purses her lips. "And now look at you, pregnant. If you would've stayed, none of this would've happened."

I clench my fists so hard, my nails bite my palms.

She pulls me inside and I'm back in the shithole.

It didn't change one bit.

Same narrow corridor. Same rotten parquet strewn with hairballs and soup bones picked clean and yellow dabs of cockroach poison. The cracked rotary dial phone sits on top of the dresser with most of its drawers missing. Above it the warped wallpaper is scribbled with phone numbers. Behind it steel hooks are driven directly into the cement wall and are overtaxed with hats, coats, and jackets. A dilapidated wardrobe yawns, its doors eaten through by woodworms, hinges broken. Numerous cardboard boxes are stuffed with rags and shoes. I see a pair of my ice skates sticking out from the same place where I put them years ago. The lamps on the ceiling have no shades, all smashed in the heat of drunken fights between mama and Lyosha, or mama and whomever she imagined while she battered the air.

There is the hustle and bustle of people trying to fit into the tight space. I edge away and lean on the wall.

"You look fat," says Sonya matter-of-factly.

"Irkadura got knocked up! Irkadura got knocked up!" Lenochka bounces up and down. Sonya smacks her and she scowls and falls quiet.

"Come in, come in." Grandma wipes her hands on her soiled apron. "I've just washed the floors." She eyes the hallway. "It's all those cursed animals. All that hair! The minute I clean up, it's dirty again. Can you believe it?" She claps her hands and tips her head back and bursts into hoarse laughter.

I don't want to see this, to listen to this.

There is breath on my back.

The boar! The boar! says the eaglet. *I want my boar!*

Yes. Yes, I remember.

I lift my head and turn, coming face to face with Lyosha.

His shirt is unbuttoned, showing his hairy chest. He grins, his piggy eyes are intoxicated. He regards me with a brazen stare that spells ownership, a hundred kilograms of pork on top of the gutted mouse.

"Holy gee," he says. "You're alive after all."

I grit my teeth. We're centimeters apart, murderous loathing on one end and bestial lust on the other. I flex my fingers, not knowing what I will do, only knowing that it will be something horrid and painful and that I can't wait anymore and I will do it right now, and just as I raise my hand, grandma grips me and plants a kiss on my cheek.

"You forgot about us. How could you? That's a bad thing to do. And who is this?" She taps on my belly and talks in an annoying childish voice. "Who is hiding in there? Ah? Who is it? Tell baba Valya."

The eaglet jabs at her hand.

"Oy! I felt it! Right there!"

I squirm out of her hold. *Let go, you stupid cockroach.*

But the moment is gone.

"What are you standing there for like a statue, to look pretty?" says Lyosha. He is shaky, acting sober. "Go ahead, undress. I want to see what you got there."

He watches me unbutton the coat. The button gets stuck in the slit and I tug at the lapel and feel a hand on mine.

Pavlik blocks Lyosha with his back. "It's okay, you're okay. Relax. I'm with you. You know, you're right. He does look like a boar."

A boar that likes to feed on mice.

Pavlik helps me to unbutton.

"Yulechka, your slippers," says Anton.

Yulia unzips her boots and carefully places them in the dingy corner by the door and straightens with a rigid smile. "There are so many of you. You have such a big family, Irina."

"Family? Where do you see a family?" Lyosha snorts. "Pigsty, that's the name for it. Five bitches and them damned animals. I'm the only man here."

"Swine." Lenochka sticks out her tongue.

"What did you say, you little whore?"

"She's not a whore," says Sonya, "and don't you dare call her names."

"Watch your mouth. You, come here!"

Lenochka hides behind her mother.

"You wait, I'll deal with you later." He takes Anton's unresisting hand and shakes it. "Kabansky, Aleksey Ivanovich. You see what I have to put up with? If I don't nip this in the bud, they'll suck out all of my blood, damned duras."

"Baboch, Anton Borisovich," says Anton slowly.

I can't stand it anymore and slink to the kitchen.

Compared to Pavlik's it feels big. Ten square meters painted dirty beige. A rickety table is pushed to the wall on the right. On its chipped formica surface sits a pot of boiled potatoes, a couple of pies, and a plate of homemade butter cookies. Grandma's work. She's the only one who cooks.

I walk to the far end and sit by the window. The fridge hums and shudders. Tabby Vaska springs from it, hissing, and dashes out. I pass my eyes over the gas stove, the laminated cabinets, their edges chipped, the sink full of dirty dishes. Everything is at once nostalgic and revolting.

Pavlik perches on the stool next to me. To his right sit Yulia and Anton, guarded. Lenochka hops in Sonya's lap. Then grandma, mama, and Lyosha. I notice a change in him I've failed to see until now. He is cleanly shaven and his hair is cropped short. A nasty suspicion lodges itself in my stomach.

Did the ravens hire you?

I crane my neck to look into the corridor, but I can't see the coat hooks from here.

Lyosha slaps his thighs and leans forward. "Holy gee, Irka! How did you manage to get pregnant?"

Off your dick, pigface.

"How it usually happens," says Pavlik mockingly, "from a stork."

I find his hand under the table.

169

"From a stork, huh?" Mama cracks up.

"From a stork!" Grandma claps her hands and tilts her head back and cackles, showing off her golden teeth. "Oy, Pavlik. You're funny."

Lenochka titters, Sonya shushes her.

"I don't understand," says Lyosha, not amused.

"Oh, it's very simple," says Pavlik. He acts comical and relaxed, but I can hear the ice beneath his words. "All the stork has to do is look at the girl, and she gets pregnant."

I hold back a smile.

"Is that what you did then, look at her?"

"Excuse me, if I may—" Anton makes to stand.

"Wait a second," says mama. "There is something I want to say first." She opens a bottle of Zhigulevskoe and takes a swig. "Irka, you're only sixteen. You could've waited. What were you thinking, huh? Look at me. If not for you, if not for your dear papochka—devil knows where he is right now—your mama might have had a career, might have had a different life. But no, that animal had to have me day and night." She takes another swig.

The silence is unbearable, broken only by chewing noises from the corner by the sink, the dogs working on soup bones.

Thank you, Mama, for your frankness.

"And what if I don't want to be a grandmother yet, did you think about that? I'm too young to be a grandmother. I have my own life to take care of, so don't you think about dropping off your brat here while you go have a good time, you hear me? And don't look at me like that. What do you want me to say, to congratulate you? Is that what you want?" She fixes her eyes on Pavlik. "And you. You stole my daughter from me. You could've at least asked me first."

"Please accept my deepest apologies, Marina Viktorovna,"

says Pavlik. "I should've done that. I'm sorry."

The air is growing hotter.

"Yeah, you should've." Mama gulps her beer.

"Well?" Lyosha stares at me. "Where is your damned pen and paper? Apologize to your mother. You've abandoned her, you left not a note, nothing! I have searched all over Moscow for you, and then I find you riding the metro like nothing happened, and you slip right through my fingers. You know what she did?" He answers Yulia's questioning face. "She kicked me in the nuts and ran!"

"If I may—" Anton tries again.

But Lyosha is not done. "You mute bitch."

Pavlik squeezes my hand.

I hear the water rumble in the kettle and I get an idea.

"Oy! The pies. The pies are getting cold. Eat the pies." Grandma giggles and grabs the plate and offers food around, trying to smooth it over.

I suddenly want to squash her like a cockroach.

"Shut up, both of you. Let him speak." Sonya nods at Anton.

"Are you telling me to shut up?" Lyosha's face darkens. "Is that what you're telling me? To shut up in my own apartment?"

"Your apartment? Listen to him."

"Watch it," he says quietly. "Don't mind them, Anton Borisovich, speak. They'll gab your ears off if you let them."

"Thank you." Anton stands, white as sheet. "I'd like to say a few words, if I may. First of all, we're grateful to you for being willing to meet us on such a short notice. We wanted to discuss the future of our children, Pavel and Irina. And, well, as this is a special occasion"—he picks up his leather briefcase—"we thought you might like a little token of appreciation for your hospitality."

He unfastens the flap, takes out a couple bottles of liquor and a box of chocolates.

Lenochka reaches for it. Sonya smacks her hand.

"Perfume for the ladies." He hands out small glass vials.

"Papa, you've outdone yourself."

"French!" Sonya pulls out the stopper and sniffs it.

"Oy! You didn't have to," Grandma titters.

Mama takes hers as if she wants to drink it.

Then there is a sizeable tin of caviar to a collective gasp, and a tube of German gumballs for Lenochka. She squeals, but Sonya snatches it and shoves it under her thigh.

Last, Anton hands Lyosha a steel flask. "This is for you, Aleksey Ivanovich."

Lyosha grunts in delight. "Now that's what I'm talking about." He opens it and waves it under his nose. "Learn, all of you. This is a man who knows how to get his business done right. To you, Anton—what was it?"

"Borisovich."

"To Anton Borisovich!" Lyosha takes a swig.

"You're welcome," says Anton dryly.

"Yes, thank you. Thank you." He belches.

"Consider it the ransom for the bride." Anton sits down.

Yulia is still, as if she's carved from wood.

Anton strokes her interlaced hands. "I propose we talk about our collective future. Of course, by future, I mean marriage."

The word settles like sediment.

The kettle boils. Grandma turns off the gas.

Should I pour it outright or make it look like an accident?

I don't care how you do it, says the eaglet. *Just get me my boar. I'm tired of waiting.*

Hold on a minute.

The eaglet hits my diaphragm.

I suppress a gasp.

Anton launches into a spiel about the wedding, what restaurant to celebrate it at, what type of car to rent, how many guests to invite, what food to order, and the cost of it all.

While he talks, everyone begins to eat. The slurping, the chewing, and the finger-sucking makes me sick. Pavlik takes one timid bite of a cabbage pie. Yulia doesn't touch a morsel and politely declines every one of grandma's offers.

"How much can you contribute?" says Anton.

Mama's mouth is full of potato. "How much what?"

"How much money can you contribute to the wedding?"

"How much do you need?"

"What are you talking about? What money?" Lyosha's lips are shiny. He's chomping down on a hunk of bread with butter and caviar. "Have them sign the certificate and be done with it. This wedding is your idea, you pay for it."

"Let me explain something," says Anton, deceptively quiet. "Irina has been living with us for the last two months without any financial assistance from you. We would certainly appreciate—"

"Fuck if we knew where she was!" Lyosha slams a fist on the table. Plates rattle.

"Lyosha, don't," says mama.

"Shut your mouth! The man of the house speaks." He lurches up. The stool falls out from under him with a clatter. "I'm the one feeding you. I'm the only one with a real job. I get paid real money, not like you, duras. What do they pay you, hardly enough for bread?" He leers at grandma.

She shrinks. "Lyosha, sit, sit, eat your pie."

"What do you do in your hospital, empty bedpans?"

I look at the kettle. Has the handle cooled down enough?

"What kind of job do you have, Aleksey Ivanovich, if you don't mind me asking?" says Yulia.

Lyosha sizes her up. "Security."

"Oh, that's great news. Irina told us you were looking for a job."

"Did she?"

"That and more," says Pavlik. "Irina also told us—"

"Oy, we forgot about the tea!" Grandma makes to get up. "Would you like some tea?"

I push on her shoulder and rise.

"Will you do it, Irka?"

I will. I stare at Lyosha.

"What are you looking at? Teach her manners, that one," he tells Pavlik. "She is a sly mouse. She is playing mute, like she's stupid, but I know stupid. She's not stupid, it's all pretense, mark my words. Put her in her place and show her who's the boss. You get what I'm saying?" He winks.

I lift the kettle off the stove. It's hot and heavy and the handle burns my fingers. I ignore the pain, grip it harder, and turn.

You're a pig and you deserve to be slaughtered, but first I will boil your dick.

I walk up to Lyosha and tip the kettle over his crotch. The lid flies off. The scalding water slops over the rim and out of the spout. My fingers are on fire and I loosen my grip on the kettle and it tumbles out of my hands.

Lyosha's eyes bulge. For a moment he doesn't make a sound, then he squeals like an injured hog, scorched and steaming. He careens and topples off the stool and—

The mouse squeaks and scurries out of the way. The boar

thunders to the floor. The catfish plops by its side, opens its huge maw, as if it wants to say something and doesn't know what. The herrings vanish. The cockroach aimlessly bustles around on its bandy legs. The viper uncoils, its forked tongue flicking. The owl hoots. And the butterfly flits to the mouse, to the viper, to the owl, and to the mouse again.

The boar roars. Its paunch is flaming red. Harsh wheezes escape its snout together with the stink of half-digested roughage. The mouse doesn't move, transfixed. It's not the scalded paunch it's looking at, it's the thing below. A twisted hunk of flesh, rubbery and limp. The mouse wants to bite it off. If only the boar didn't twitch, if only it lay still.

The cockroach stops running around and busies itself between the boar's hind legs. It excretes some kind of a paste and rubs it in. The boar quiets down, relieved, and that's when the mouse bares its sharp little teeth and springs. The butterfly flies in its way. The mouse dodges it. So close, so close, it can see the blistering skin when the cockroach swings around and blocks it. The owl pecks at the mouse and the viper hisses, and they hustle the mouse away but not before it bites the cockroach with a satisfying crunch.

CHAPTER TWENTY-ONE

HORSE

I sit on a box, resting. I'm sore. We've been packing all week. Today we move to Margarita's apartment. It's her wedding gift to us. She said she wants us to start our own family in our own place, but Pavlik told me there is more to it. She hasn't been the same since that murder in the flat across the landing. She's been having dizziness spells, her blood pressure has spiked, and the other day she fell down the stairs. Yulia wants her here, to watch over her.

I've got someone to watch over me. The ravens.

Pavlik refuses to admit that he's gotten any more death threats, and I refuse to believe him. His face is frightened and peaked, and there are dark circles under his eyes. He stacks the last of the books in a box, closes the flaps, plops on the floor, and surveys the room.

I follow his gaze.

Everything has been emptied. The bookcases and the dresser and the desk and the bed. Stacks of boxes line the wall, and when Pavlik coughs from the dust, the noise he makes is gutted and echoey.

"You know, I still can't believe that you did it. When you tipped the kettle, I thought, no way. It just slipped out of her hand. I mean, if it were me, I wouldn't have the guts, Irina. If I came across one of them, say, on the street somewhere, I couldn't do it, couldn't hurt him or even say anything. I'd get paralyzed." He lifts his eyes.

I regard him wearily. We've been through this so many times, I've lost count. He just can't stop talking about it.

"Didn't"—he glances at the door—"he ever make you feel paralyzed?"

I nod. *Every single time.*

"Listen, I'm worried about you. What if he threatens you when he gets out of the hospital? I don't think they'll keep him there longer than a week."

A raven croaks behind the window.

I flinch, suddenly angry, and cut across my neck with the edge of my palm. *I'll slit his throat with a kitchen knife.* Words bubble up in me and surge in my mouth and die, dry and broken.

Pavlik shakes his head. "Please. You're not serious, are you?"

I repeat the gesture.

"You're scaring me, Irina. Look, I understand how you feel, but all of this fantasizing aside, if he attacks you, you won't stand a chance. The man is huge. I can't be by your side at all times, I simply can't."

You don't need to. I'll be fine on my own.

"And even if I was, it's not like I'd be much help. Think about it. He'll squish me like a bug. Or, in your words, like a butterfly." He smiles at me sadly.

I reach for the bag that Yulia gave me, unzip it, take out the notebook and write. "The boar may be a big bully, but it's a coward. The second I threaten it with a knife, it'll shit itself. My only regret is that I didn't realize it sooner."

Pavlik looks at it, shocked. "Do you really mean this?"

And for a moment I abhor his fragility, his gayness.

"Yes. I will fight it. I will fight them all. The ravens. The eels. I will fight them until—"

Several ravens scream at once. A jackal howls as if in answer. I tear to the window and draw the curtain aside. The steely sky is boiled with clouds. There is no sign of the sun, only a uniform grayness. And down below, on the naked elm, they sit, covering it entirely.

I recoil.

"What is it?"

"The ravens. About a hundred."

Pavlik peers out. "I see only one." He studies me for a tense moment. "You mean, it feels to you like it's a hundred?"

I grab my head. I want to ram it through the glass. It takes me a moment to calm down. I pick up the notebook and fish the pen from under the radiator. "Something bad will happen today. I can feel it. Pretend like you're sick, invent something, I don't know, say you have a headache or a stomachache."

"How do you know?"

"I don't. I just have a funny feeling, like I had about the goat that got hit by the ravens, remember?"

A long yowl in the street.

"Did you hear that?" I can't write fast enough. "The jackal, just now. It must be nearby."

"Shakalov is at the theater prepping it for the season opening. That was a dog, Irina," says Pavlik carefully.

"I'm not mad! I simply have this—" I nibble on the pen. "First comes a noise, an animal noise, like a harbinger. Then I see them, the beasts, in the streets, on the roofs, or in the place where something will happen."

A rap on the door.

I vigorously shake my head.

Anton peeks in. "Are you ready?"

"Yes, I think we are."

I punch the notepad in frustration.

"There are sandwiches in the kitchen. Help yourselves. I'll go and warm up the car." Anton leaves.

I hurl the notebook after him. It hits the door and slides down in a rustle of pages.

"Is something wrong?"

I glare at him.

Pavlik backs away. "You terrify me."

I terrify myself.

"Let's have some tea. It'll make you feel better." He puts on his well-mannered theater face.

And I feel empty. Pregnant but empty.

I trail after him into the kitchen and watch him fuss around me. He puts two plates on the table and takes out two sandwiches from the fridge and pours tea and drops in sugar cubes and slides in spoons. He rattles about how excited he is to move, to live in his own place, away from his parents' constant overbearance.

I don't really listen, as I bite into the sandwich and chew it. The cold bologna tastes like rubber and the bread tastes like dirt. I finish it, wash the plate, stick it in the dryer rack, dress, and follow Pavlik outside.

It's biting cold. Heaps of blackened snow line the road. The yard rebounds with the usual Sunday din. Children's calls, shouts, and dogs barking. I look at the elm. It's bare. I watch for motion, for any movement in the shadows or in the open doorways. There is nothing.

I stay by the car.

It takes Pavlik and Anton several trips up and down five stories to haul all the boxes and stack them in the trunk and on the back seat with barely any room left for me. By the time they're done, my toes and fingers are numb and my face is burning.

An hour later we're at Margarita's place.

I get out and cover my ears. There is a loud screeching and rustling and scraping of talons.

They're here, hiding and waiting.

Yell at them, says the eaglet. *Drive them into the open.*

I can't. And don't you try kicking me again.

I will. The eaglet jabs me.

I gasp for breath. *Is that the way of it now?*

It is, until you feed me. I'm hungry.

"See? Everything is fine," says Pavlik.

The sound of his voice makes me flinch.

"I don't know what you were worried about." His eyes sparkle, so black in the cold. Plumes of breath escape his mouth. He gestures at the empty yard, the broken swings, the benches.

A bum wobbles along the sidewalk, gaunt and emaciated. An earflap hat covers half of his bony face and his pants are tied with a rope to stop them from falling. A quilted jacket hangs on his shoulders like on a rake.

A horse, a homeless downtrodden horse. And I know what will happen. *They will maul it.*

"Pavlusha! Come here, son. You take this one and I'll get the TV."

I have an urge to yank on Pavlik's arm, to point out the bum to him, to write, to explain, then it's gone. Convincing him will only make me lose time.

All right, eaglet. I know what to do.

Do you?

Watch me.

I spin on my heels and march to the entranceway.

"Irina, wait!"

They catch up to me by Margarita's apartment.

"Why didn't you wait for us?"

"Irina, get back to the car. We can't leave it unattended." Anton is irritated.

The door opens. I rush past Yulia, straight to the kitchen. Any minute now, any minute. I'll be late. I yank open drawer after drawer and rummage inside.

In the corridor Yulia is scandalized. "You left the car unattended?"

"Only for a few minutes, Mama."

"Anton, you'll strain your back like this!"

"I got this, Yulechka, I got this."

And I hear it happening.

It takes me by surprise. The breaking of the glass and the snapping of the bones and the neighing and the whinnying and the croaking. The ravens strike the horse and fell it and I scream a cry of dismay.

I'm late!

"Irina!" Pavlik is in the kitchen. "What happened? Why are you screaming?"

I close my mouth with an audible click.

I'm coming to get you, bastards.

I find what I'm looking for in the top drawer by the stove—a big steak knife, its blade worn, and its wooden handle polished with use. I snatch it, push past Pavlik, past all of them gathered in the doorway, and rush down the stairs and into the street. My arm outstretched, I sprint across the road to Anton's Lada and halt, wheezing, clasping my belly.

Go ahead, eaglet. Say it.

Behind me are running footsteps.

"Oh God." Pavlik pries my fingers off the knife. There is no need for it anymore, so I let him.

On the blackened snow lies the bum, face up. Blood runs from his fleshy nose. He has swarthy skin and his features are coarse and exaggerated. His hair is a matted heap of what once were black shiny curls.

Ethnic cleansing at its finest. Let's butcher a homeless Jew to show our might. Russia for the Russians, is that what you ravens chant? Fury grips me. I look for a note. They must have left one, they must have.

Anton cradles his head. "My car! My car!"

It's destroyed. The windows are jagged holes. The tires are slashed. The trunk gapes open, its lock gouged out like an eye. Everything of value has been taken: the VCR, the computer, the radio and cassette tower with both speakers. The boxes of clothes and books have been dragged out and torn, their contents spilled around.

"I'm calling militia."

"Don't waste your breath. Better call the ambulance." Pavlik squats next to the bum, shakes him, asks for his name.

I see a white corner sticking out of his pant pocket and pull it out. Same paper, same handwriting.

PAVEL BABOCH, PANSY JEW. A TASTE OF WHAT'S COMING.

I hand it to Pavlik. Our eyes meet and his pupils widen.

Will you believe me now?

"What's this?" Anton takes the note.

I glare at him. *A purge message, Russia or death.*

A small speculating crowd gathers around us. Muffled whisperings are exchanged, theories about what might have happened, who did it and why and how. The cost of replacing the windows and the tires. Who is to blame for the crime increase in Moscow and in the country on the whole.

I help Pavlik gather up our things.

Shortly after we tie up what we manage to salvage in blankets, the ambulance shows up. The medics roll the bum onto the stretcher and depart. An army-green Kamaz truck labors into the yard. A bald driver hops out, and after a brief conversation with Anton and an exchange of cash, he tows away the Lada.

At last we are ushered back into Margarita's apartment where it's warm and where we sip tea in the kitchen and I trace on Pavlik's palm, "Sim."

He studies me. He can't really say anything under Yulia's sharp eyes.

Who else? Who else will you listen to?

He nods.

The doorbell chimes. Militia is here. Yulia goes out to greet them.

"I'm sorry I didn't believe you."

It's okay. I'm having a hard time believing myself.

CHAPTER TWENTY-TWO

RAVENS

I run after Pavlik up the steps of the underpass. It's a quarter past nine. We slept in, exhausted by all of the questioning, and now we're late. We sprint along the sidewalk and halt by the crossing. I stoop and wheeze and clutch my sides. My belly is getting heavy. Sweat trickles down my face, so I wipe it off with the back of my hand. The light turns green, the cars don't move, and we have to weave in and out of them to get to the other side.

"Look," says Pavlik. "Pensioners on the promenade."

I turn my head.

About a hundred meters up the street marches the reason for the stalled traffic, a rally, a dark mass of people holding up signs with slogans and pennants and Soviet flags. A shrill voice shouts through a megaphone.

"For Motherland! For Stalin!"

"For government's resignation!"

"Death to capitalism!"

"Off with unemployment!"

A pair of retired women head the procession. They hold up a red banner with semi-profiles of Stalin and Lenin, cheek to cheek, like newlyweds gazing into a bright socialist future.

Fucking communist party supporters. Mules, too dumb to think. Let's resurrect the dead so they can solve my problems for me—save me from poverty, impotence, and fear—because I'm too lazy to do jack-shit on my own.

Distracted, I stumble on the curb. Pavlik catches me. We draw away from the tide of bystanders, bolt along the street, under the archway, around the theater, and crash through the back door.

A sense of unease smothers me.

"Who is it?"

"It's us, Ilinichna." Pavlik catches his breath. "It's us."

She clambers out of the booth. "Ah! Pavlik? Irina? You scared the devil out of me. Hurry up, he's waiting."

"I know," Pavlik pants. "How long?"

"About an hour now. He's furious, you hear me?" She grins at me from behind her oversized glasses. "Ah, so it's true what I heard? Congratulations!"

I smile and nod and unbutton my coat. My shirt is sticking to my back and my face is sweltering hot and I have an urge to get back out onto the street. The theater air suffocates me. It's ominously quiet.

"Did you hear what happened?" says Ilinichna conspiratorially.

"Please, not right now." Pavlik pulls on my hand.

"Shakalov got sacked."

We exchange a glance.

"He did? When?"

"This very morning. Now go, go! I'll tell you more later. You don't want to anger him any more." She waves us to the stairs.

Shakalov is gone. I should feel happy, I should beam. Instead, I skid down the steps after Pavlik. Everything about the theater I came to love—Ilinichna with her turtle clumsiness and cookies and tea, the actors' posters on the walls, the smell of the velvet draperies and the makeup and the dust—all feels wrong.

It's too quiet, I don't like it.

We enter the auditorium. It's vast, dark, and hushed. The curtains are drawn. The lights are turned off except for a handful of projectors over the stage. In the front row sits the hunched figure of Sim, a sequined scarf about his neck, his hands interlaced. He doesn't raise his head as we approach, doesn't indicate he heard us, his eyes cast down.

"You're late," he says to the floor.

"I'm sorry, Sim. We—"

"Pavlik, my child." He looks up. His eyes are tired, his whole face is sunken. "When did I tell you to be here?"

"At nine a.m., but—"

"And what time is it now?"

"Sim, please, let me—"

"Silence! I don't want to hear any excuses. Why didn't you tell me right away, right when it started?"

Blood drains out of Pavlik's face. "Why didn't I tell you what?"

Oh no, no, no. I slap my forehead. *Don't do this.*

"You know exactly what I mean."

"I'm sorry, I'm not sure—"

"The notes. The threatening notes. I want to know when

186

you got the first one."

Pavlik takes a step back. "Honestly, I don't know what you're talking about, Sim. There was only one, the one that we got yesterday—"

"Don't lie to me."

Thin silence spreads over the stage. I watch the dust dance in the light and feel my stomach twist tighter.

"Do you want to get shot?"

Pavlik flinches. "No."

"Then talk to me."

It takes him a moment, then he says to the floor, "In December, that day you dropped us off after—"

"What did it say?"

"Something about...Kostya forgetting to tell me—"

"You're next, Jewish homo."

Pavlik's eyes widen. "Who told you?"

"Nobody told me anything. They send me notes like that on every holiday. I get particularly nasty ones on my birthday, promising to rip my Jewish ass in two. They're not very elaborate, I must say, rather primitive and to the point." He suddenly looks at me. "Did you know about this, Irina?"

I want to slip through the floor.

"Why didn't you tell me?"

"Sim, we didn't want to bother you—"

"Bother me?" His face darkens. "Do you understand what this means? I've already lost—"

"I know!" Pavlik's voice bounds to the ceiling, high-strung and upset. "You don't need to remind me!"

"Come here. Sit with me."

Pavlik reluctantly walks over to Sim.

I lower myself onto the edge of the seat by his side. It's so quiet that the silence makes my ears ring. I strain to listen to any trace of any noise I can detect, and I hear something faint, some scratching, like the claws of a dog on the wooden floor. I spin around and scan the darkness. Nothing.

"What do you want me to do?"

"You're an actor. You have given yourself to the theater, you must keep performing, keep creating."

"But how, Sim, how? How can I perform when I can't even be myself? When I can't even tell my own father..." He hides his face.

"Go on."

"It doesn't matter."

"I want to hear you say it."

Pavlik shakes his head.

"What are you afraid of?"

"Of being harassed," he whispers. "Beaten. Killed."

I slip my hand into his.

"Listen to me. I understand how you feel. You think I'm not afraid? I am afraid, very much so. It's okay to be afraid, but don't let it stop you. That's what they want, for you to tuck your tail and to stay quiet. What would happen if we all did that?"

Pavlik shrugs.

"This"—Sim spreads his arms—"all of this, the theater, the plays we stage here, it's our way of changing our country, this savage place we've been born into. And don't you ever be afraid of who you are. Everything in you has a right to live, to be free and to be beautiful." Sim lifts Pavlik's face. "Listen to me. Listen carefully. The moment you stop creating, you die. Not when you're killed. When you're killed, only your body is gone, your art will live on."

"And what's it to you? What's my life to you? Why do you care?" Pavlik's eyes well up with water.

"Come here." Sim pulls him close and buries Pavlik's face

in the folds of the scarf. Pavlik's shoulders shake. Sim strokes his head, fatherly almost. "Shhh. Cry it out, crying is good for you. I miss Kostya, too. I miss him very much."

Movement catches my eye, by the curtain, high up under the ceiling. Something stirs in the shadow. I peer up and see nothing, and that's when I hear it: muffled croaking outside the theater building.

The ravens.

I spring up. The cushioned seat behind me folds with a soft thud.

Why did I tell Pavlik to see Sim? Why?

I ripple with guilt and shame and regret and horror. Awful horror. It shoots down my spine and slides inside my stomach and drives all blood down to my feet. I pull the bundle from the sleeve of my coat and unwrap it.

You won't catch me unaware this time.

I hide the knife behind my back and take hold of Pavlik's arm.

"What is it?"

I mime and make noises.

"Some kind of a bird? A vulture?"

I shake my head and try again and croak.

"Ravens? Those same...ravens?"

I nod.

"Are you sure?"

I give him the look that makes him grab his hair. "They're coming here?"

They already are.

"Now?"

"Is that a kitchen knife?" says Sim.

I edge back and mount the steps to the stage and survey the hall, straining to hear any noise, any disturbance. My heart thumps in my mouth and my saliva tastes metallic. Darkness solidifies, impatient, hungry.

We're trapped. The theater is closed for mid-season break, so there is only us and Ilinichna. They'll intercept us if we try to get out. I bet Shakalov still has all the keys.

Pavlik is frantic. "Sim, we need to get out of here."

"Why? What is going on? Irina, get off the stage and give me that knife before you poke your eye out."

"Sim, please. Irina can sense things, right before they happen. First she hears an animal noise, then—"

"Sense things? What are you talking about? What things?"

"Please, there's no time! The Nationalists are coming here, they'll be here any minute!"

"Is that true, Irina?" Sim measures me with a heavy look. "Is that true, what Pavlik is saying?"

I don't respond, I can't even nod. Dread spreads over me. They're inside the building. I hear their rustling wings and scraping claws. The ravens and a jackal.

Come here then, scum, come and show me your real faces.

There is movement in my belly, a faint kick.

Eaglet?

"They're here," says Pavlik.

Running footsteps reverberate along the halls.

Eaglet, talk to me.

Silence.

They're coming, eaglet! The ravens!

Nothing an eagle can't kill, says the eaglet.

I'm not an eagle!

You're not a mouse either.

Who am I then?

Who do you want to be?

They enter through the doorway. A pack of young guys in

black coats, black caps, and black gloves, Shakalov in the back.

"Who are you and what are you doing in my theater?" Bellows Sim, then he sees him. "Vladimir Kuzmich? What a surprise. I thought I asked you to vacate the premises this morning."

Shakalov doesn't answer. He looks scared and he avoids Sim's gaze. "Go ahead, boys, do them. Quickly and quietly."

"What's all this about?" says Sim calmly.

"Don't listen to him, do them!"

"Do us?" Sim chuckles. "What is this, a farce? Ten boys against an old man and two children?"

Shakalov shouts, "Now!"

It happens very fast.

We're swarmed with bodies. An arm flies up with a truncheon that's usually used by militants. A blunt whack, and Sim topples to the floor and takes the hitter with him. Pavlik gets wrangled and pinned to the wall.

"Run!" he yells at me.

I'm not going anywhere, I'm done running. I bound off the stage and charge. Somebody sticks out a foot. I sprawl, and the knife flies out of my hand. Arms catch me and position me in front of Pavlik.

"Don't touch her! Can't you see she's pregnant?"

"Pregnant with a Jewish freak," says someone, "from a Jewish faggot." A jitter of laughter.

"Let her go!"

Shakalov's breath is on my neck. "Watch, whore."

Arms work on Pavlik like pistons with sounds of flat impact. His face changes. His eyes open wider and the fear is gone from them, replaced with reckless daring. "Vladimir Kuzmich! Does it excite you to watch a bunch of guys beat up a fairy?"

CHAPTER TWENTY-TWO

"Shut him up," Shakalov spits.

Pavlik forces a laugh. "Is that what you're afraid of? My words? I'll give you more." He begins to fight back, clumsily at first, then fueled with some insane abandon. He hooks a man closest to him and sends him flying, clips another, and all this time he keeps yelling. "Are you a voyeur, Vladimir Kuzmich? Do you get hard watching men fuck?" His punches grow weaker under the blows. There are simply too many of them, and they quickly recover from the shock of him resisting.

"You guys like hitting me? Go ahead, hit me more, I'll moan for you." A gloved hand swipes at his mouth. He spits blood. "You don't get laid much, do you?" The breath gets knocked out of him. He doubles over, raises his face. "I understand...girls won't have you. That's why you want me so bad...that's why—" A blow cuts him off.

"This is a lesson for you, for fucking Jewish trash." Shakalov speaks in my ear. "How did he do it, tell me. Did he wank off in a napkin and stick it up your cunt?" His hand moves down between my buttocks.

Pavlik's face lifts one more time, bloody and disfigured. His eyes find me. "I'm sorry..." A kick, and he slumps to the floor.

"Looks like your lover boy has taken the hint." Shakalov feels me about.

Rage grips me, blind and overwhelming.

I hope you die, you petty chauvinistic shit.

I ram my heel into his crotch. He gasps and releases me. I spot the knife under a seat, lunge for it, swirl around, stab him and miss. Two guys rush at me. I snarl and brandish the blade around. They start back, surprised.

"Bitch!" Shakalov straightens, his face contorted with pain. "Put that away, before I carve your face with it!"

I push forth with my belly, daring them.

Go on, hit me! Hit me! The words are on my tongue, by my teeth. They want to spill, but instead of speech a string of unintelligible noises breaks through, like the screech of an eagle.

They eye me, uncertain.

"She's crazy."

"Finish her," says Shakalov.

"But, Vladimir Kuzmich, she's pregnant."

"I said, finish her!"

I lunge at him. He catches my wrist and twists it. The knife drops, something sharp hits my head, and I fall.

CHAPTER TWENTY-THREE

COWS

I dream about having my baby. The doctor pulls something warm from between my legs and hands it to me, a squirmy squealing thing sticky with gore. It has a large ugly head and a hirsute body. A newborn boar. Its piggy eyes fasten on me. It sniffs me and latches on to my breast. I drop it and wake up, screaming, on a bed in a brightly lit room filled with hospital smell. A hand pats me. It belongs to a nurse with a dull round face.

I jerk up.

She pushes me back. "Lie still."

Pavlik!

"So stubborn. I said, lie still! You'll make it worse for your kid. Here, let me..." She lifts me by the armpits and fluffs up the pillow behind me. "Better?"

I moan. Every muscle hurts and every bone is as brittle as glass. My head is stuffed with cotton, my throat is parched. I try to swallow and I can't. Something prickles my arm. An IV is hooked to my vein. I shift my feet and I feel a warm gurgling plastic bag with a catheter snaking up my leg.

"Measure your temperature." The nurse hands me a thermometer and departs to the next bed. "Larisa, wake up. Temperature."

"What's the hurry, Lida? I'm sleeping. Just write that it's normal."

"If you want to complain, you go ahead and complain to Nikita Matveich, not to me. I spit on your temperature. Understand? Take it."

Larisa grumbles.

I look around.

The room is small and narrow. Four beds, two by either wall, sweaty window curtained off by drapes printed with brown flowers. Flowers everywhere, on the oilcloth floor, on the bedding, on the towels, on the robes. And women, pregnant women, like bloated cows sitting in dead blooms.

On the bed next to mine reclines Larisa. She is in her thirties and she is huge. Her skin is milky white and freckled and her swollen legs are wrapped in elastic bandage. She shakes out the thermometer. The bedsprings whine in protest. "I took it yesterday and it was just fine. Why the hell do I need to measure it every day? Tell me, Galya." She addresses the girl on the bed across from her.

The nurse slams the door.

I flinch. The women don't react, as if it's normal.

"What do I know? I'm not a doctor." Galya is bony and barely twenty. Her eyes are suspicious and her oily hair is pulled into a ponytail. She's wrapped in a pink robe with daisies. "Hey, new girl! What's your name?"

What do you care?

She walks over and plops onto my bed. "I'm Galya. This is Larisa. She's having twins. Isn't she huge?"

"Thank God it's not triplets." Larisa snorts. "Egor would've killed me."

"And that's Natasha over there."

Natasha says nothing. She has a broad, pimply face, callous, the type that doesn't smile lightly.

They all study me, waiting for me to say something.

"Why won't you talk?" says Galya.

You want my life story? I'll give it to you. By the time I'm done, you'll be puking out your guts.

"Maybe she's deaf," says Larisa.

"I don't know. She's not saying anything." Galya shrugs. "Can you talk?"

I nod and go through my usual pantomime. Moving hurts.

"Oh, you're mute?"

Can you leave me alone now?

"But you're not deaf. That's weird. Why are you mute?"

If you won't shut up, I'll strip off this heinous robe and stuff it down your throat. My head pounds and my stomach cramps. *What did they do to you, Pavlik?*

"How far along are you? You look awfully small."

When I don't react, she shakes me. "How many months?"

I show her six fingers.

"I thought so."

"Why the hell did they put her in here?" says Larisa. "This is gynecology. They should've put her in obstetrics."

"The clinic is full, that's why," says Natasha. "Leave her alone. Can't you see she's in pain?"

They quarrel.

After a while, it turns to white noise and I doze off.

I come to in the evening.

Natasha is gone. The stained mattress on her bed is stripped. Larisa snores. Helpful Galya hops over.

"You missed the doctor. He said he'll keep you here for a while, to prevent preterm labor. What did you do, fall down the stairs or what?"

Worse. Fell out of the wrong pair of legs. I turn away, as much as the IV permits.

"Don't want to talk to me? Fine. Have it your way." Galya retreats back to her bed. "I'm not planning to stay at your side and retell you every bit of news. Just so you know."

I chip flecks of paint off the wall, sullen.

Hospital, again.

My stomach is a hard rock. I can't get up, can't call anyone to find out about Pavlik, can't escape, and my baby is in danger of premature birth.

Eaglet.

It's quiet.

Eaglet, can you hear me?

No movement, not a stir. It's like I'm carrying a stone.

Eaglet, please, talk to me. I peel off a sliver of paint and hook my nail under the edge of another.

Eaglet, say something.

Nothing.

Please.

My tears roll and pool on the pillow and soak it and I drift to sleep.

The merciless shine of fluorescent lamps awakens me. It looks like the morning of the next day. Nurse Lida doles out thermometers. Larisa and Galya chat over bowls of porridge. A new girl occupies Natasha's bed. She's my age, acned and lopsided and swathed in a robe mottled with kitschy orange flowers.

I avert my eyes, glad I'm in the standard hospital-issued gown, washed out and colorless. I prop myself up. The needle in my vein hurts like an old bruise. The IV bottle is empty. A plate of buckwheat kasha, a glass of tea, and a plastic bag sit on my nightstand. I lift the bag. It crinkles.

Larisa and Galya pause their chatter.

Mandarins, a whole kilogram of mandarins.

A square of paper underneath it says, "Irina Myshko, 8th floor, room 714."

I unfold it.

"Dear Irina! I'm very worried about you. The doctor said you need rest and no visits are allowed. Pavlusha is in critical care with two broken ribs, bruised lungs, and a concussion. Sim is at home and feeling better. He sends his greetings. It's very cold outside. It takes me two hours to get from Pavlusha's hospital to yours. How are you feeling? I hope the baby is okay. Please, write. Yulia."

I read it again and again. My fingers betray me. The note slips out and floats to the floor.

Galya picks it up. "Bad news?"

I look up, unseeing.

She hands it to me. "You have no face on you. Do want something to write with?"

I taste salt on my lips and wipe my eyes.

Galya gives me a page torn out from a lined school

notebook and a pencil. "Here."

I wait for my hand to steady. "Dear Yulia! I'm feeling fine, the baby is fine. I'm very worried about Pavlik." I think a bit and add, "Please tell him I love him. Irina."

Galya hovers over my shoulder. "Who is Pavlik, your husband?"

"She's got no band, can't you see?" says Larisa.

They squabble. Larisa insists that wearing a wedding ring is a must, Galya says that nowadays it doesn't matter and calls her old-fashioned. The new girl joins in and they discuss marriage and divorce and alimony and how all men are bastards anyway, sticking it in and out and leaving the suffering of childbirth to the women. Then they tell me that I'm due for magnesium shots, to relax my abdomen muscles. They say it hurts like a motherfucker and that I won't be able to sit for hours. When I get the shots, after the nurse leaves, I grit my teeth and triumphantly sit up, to prove them wrong.

They all leave me in the space of three days. First goes Larisa, in the middle of the night, cursing Egor at every contraction, then Galya the next morning, then Yana, the new girl, crying and complaining loudly, all of them to the delivery ward on the floor below. They send me folded notes with babies' names, weights, heights, labor stories, well wishes, and phone numbers. New women come and go.

I stay in the hospital for two months. My days are filled with shots, tests, and gynecological examinations. After the first two weeks, I was able to stand on my own and wobble to the toilet to empty my pissbag; a week later, I could walk to the cafeteria, and now I'm well enough to stroll around the ward for hours, envious of women by the pay phones, watching their painted mouths spit bits of conversations and gasps and giggles.

You know who you are, Irina Myshko? You're not a mouse and you're not an eagle, you're just a dumb mute dura. You've never talked and you never will.

The eaglet doesn't answer me anymore. I exist through written notes from Yulia about Pavlik's improvement and through my nightly trips to the roof, to gaze down at the ground, from the height of eight floors.

At night I wait for the clinic to grow quiet, throw on my coat, step into hospital slippers, and creep out of the room. Nurses chat at their station. I hear the echo of their laughter, sneak by the elevators, slowly climb up the rickety service ladder, and push open the trapdoor. It's never locked.

I clamber onto the scratchy bitumen on my fours and stand up, legs wide apart for balance. It's March now and it smells of spring. The snow has mostly melted. Cold wind whips my hair and chills my face and I wrap my coat around me tighter.

The black sky flickers with stars. I scan the monotone carpet of roofs and walk up to the flat parapet that comes up to my shins and look down. Rare cars crawl along the street in weak streetlight. A blaring militia speeds by.

Eaglet?

All I hear is the sound of absence.

I've failed you, eaglet.

No answer. No stir.

I don't know who I am anymore, and I don't think I care. There is nothing left of me. Nothing.

I wait.

Then I hit my stomach until my knuckles hurt.

I can't live like this! Don't you understand?

I wait again.

There is only the hum of the wind.

I'm sorry, eaglet. I'm sorry.

I step onto the parapet.

The parking lot below is dimly lit and mostly empty, save for a truck and a few ambulance vans.

All I have to do is lean and fall.

Lean.

And fall.

CHAPTER TWENTY-FOUR

MOSQUITOES

I stand in the wind and sway a little and think. Eight floors. Is it high enough to guarantee death? Will the impact kill both of us or will one of us live on with terrible injuries and deformities? Cursing everything and everyone? Or will I grow wings and fly like an eagle?

"Hey!"

I give a start.

A medic stands by the ambulance van. From the roof he looks like a mosquito. He waves his arms and yells something in that pesky, annoying whine that doesn't sound like words. I get angry at being interrupted.

Come a little closer. I will jump on you and I will make you splat.

He puts hands to his mouth. The wind shifts, and I can catch the end of a phrase: "Down!" Then something else, then again, "Down!" And then, "Dura!"

I step back and stumble and fall on my ass and cry out. My tailbone connects with the hard surface and sends a bolt of pain up my spine. Rough bitumen scrapes skin off my palms and I blow on them and lick off the blood. By the time I manage to pull myself upright and regain my balance, the medic climbs out of the trapdoor.

"Wait!"

I run, one hand on my belly, another pressed to my chest. My old bra won't fit me anymore and, anyway, no bras are allowed in the hospital. In the time I was here my breasts grew two sizes bigger and stretched out, and with every step they jiggle like hot, heavy sacks of fat. I almost fall, right myself, and reach the opposite edge of the roof and pant. There is nowhere else to go.

That's it, now they'll put you in the nuthouse.

I trot to the concrete box of the elevator shaft and hide behind it and lean on the scratchy wall and wait. I can't take another step. My abdomen cramps and I double over and gasp for air that coasts in and out of my lungs like fire.

Then he's on me, scared out of his mind; on his smoky breath are vicious curses and reproaches and rebukes. They blend into the fuzzy noise of a mosquito buzz. I feel his callused hands pry me from the lift housing, lead me to the trapdoor, and help me down into another pair of hands, and one more. Two men, two medics. My shaking hands slip off the ladder rungs and my slippers slide and both men nearly collapse under my weight and scold me, terrified and relieved.

They prop me on their shoulders and I blunder between them, half-hanging, into a whirr of hushed, worried voices. I'm too fatigued to respond to anything or anyone—doctors, nurses, patients. They swarm around me in a thick cloud. Hungry mosquitoes. They question me and poke me and sting me. They hustle me into my room and get me back in my bed. Someone forces open my mouth and makes me swallow pills. Someone else puts a hot-water bottle on my stomach. Someone covers me with a blanket. The drone of their talking lulls me, and I relax and warm up and drift off and—

The mouse is covered with mosquitoes. They puncture its skin and gorge on its blood, their transparent abdomens fill with dark oozy—

I jerk awake. I suffocate under too many blankets. I fight them. My feet get tangled in the cotton cover and my arms are weak and at last I succeed in throwing them off and—

The mouse is gutted. The shiny coils of its viscera are spilled all over sticky soaked sheets. The eaglet is gone. It has been yanked out and ripped to pieces by the ravens. The mosquitoes alight on the mouse, on the edges of its torn flesh, and fold their delicate wings and probe around and pierce its hide and suck and suck and inject thinning saliva that burns and stings like acid and—

I'm hot, sweaty, and feverish.

"Temperature forty-one and rising," says a voice. "If it doesn't drop in an hour or so..."

A cold wet towel touches my face. I flinch and seize it and

fling it off me and—

The mouse is growing a pair of wings. They puncture its back and tear its hide and crackle as they grow and unfold and sprout feathers. The mouse edges off the bed and flaps them once and plummets down to the floor. Some big dark beast whacks its skull with a heavy paw and seizes it and plops it back onto the bed, and an eddy of mosquitoes descend on the mouse in a humming coat and crowd its exposed womb and feed on the tender flesh inside, their eyes small and glossy and their bodies twitchy. The noise changes and expands and more parasites fill the room and attack the mouse. Horseflies and woodpeckers and ravens and vultures and—

The lights turn on. I wince. Lenin, dressed in a white lab coat, enters the room and sits on my bed.

"Ay-ay, citizen Myshko. Ay-ay. You mustn't take your life. You must give it to the Communist Party. You must live on. Have you given any thought as to what you will do with the rest of it? Are you deaf, citizen? Are you listening?" He shakes me until my eyeballs roll around my head like pulsing marbles.

"You must believe in the Soviet power! Unquestionably!"

Two more voices join his. Karl Marx appears on Lenin's left side, Stalin on his right.

"Devotedly!"

"Blindly!"

They commiserate with me in a cold, dispassionate way, wish me a speedy recovery, line up by the bed across from me, and sing some Soviet song. A howl mixes in, that of a jackal. A chorus of jackals. They jump in through the window and surround me, stripping off my robe with their teeth and licking off my sweat with their coarse reddish tongues. Then maggots begin dropping on me from the ceiling. A rain of soft, pinkish lumps wrapped in jittering membranes. The jackals open their maws and catch them and pop them between their teeth.

I bend over the edge of the bed and throw up.

Someone wipes it—no, something. It's a tapeworm. It slurps up my vomit and glides on the slime and twists and twirls as if it wants more.

I retch but nothing comes out except a long dripping line of sour spittle. My heart drums. Sweat drips off my face.

There is a choke and a gurgle and the restroom door bursts open and the floor floods with swampy water. It stinks of mold and septic reek, the perfect breeding ground for mosquitoes. Animals slosh through it, hordes of them. Eels snake up to my feet, vipers and rats. Catfish and herrings and salamanders. The cacophony they produce is unbelievable.

Then one guttural roar rips through.

It's the boar.

I shriek.

A hand covers my mouth and I bite it and thrash. Arms pin me down. A needle bites into my vein and cold liquid bores through my arm to my heart. The edges of my vision curl, bubble, and break.

Solid darkness.

Far off shines a tiny spot of light. It sits in the middle of a freshly plowed fallow. The smell of damp, overturned earth fills my nostrils. Moist, soft, and crumbly. I fall to my knees and crawl forward and soon I reach it, a white swaddled shape.

A baby, a newborn baby. My boy.

He opens his eyes, brown and sad.

"I'm dying," he says.

"No!" I say, and I hear myself talk. I hear myself talk. "You can't die. You haven't even been born."

"I'm sorry."

"You can't leave me." I brush the dirt off my hands and touch his cheek, so smooth, so warm. Tears spill down my face. I don't care to wipe them. "Please, don't go. I don't have anyone else. How will I live without you?"

"I don't know. Live the best you can, I guess." He sighs. "I don't have much time. I thought I'd say goodbye. I thought I'd ask for something special. Can you hold me?"

I pick him up, so light and fragile, and I press him to my breast and rock him a little and whisper, "Why? Why are you leaving me? What have I done wrong?"

"Nothing," he says. "I'll be going."

"No!"

He looks at me hard. "You want me to stay?"

"Yes. Please."

"Why?"

"Because I love you."

"I don't believe you."

His words punch my chest and I can't draw a breath, and for a moment, I can't speak. "Why not?"

"How can you love something so ugly? So heinous? How can you love something spawned by the one you hate?"

I shrug. "I just do."

"No, you don't. You wanted to jump off the roof and kill me."

The light goes out of him.

"Irina Myshko, you have visitors."

I stir and wade through layers of gauze and fog and sit up, confused and groggy. The dream is leaving me fast. I snatch at its bits, at the tails of its thoughts, and in my hands it disintegrates into nothing. All I have left is an acidic taste in my mouth and a bad feeling.

Eaglet?

It's quiet.

Eaglet, answer me.

I hold a rock in my hands, a dead rock wrapped in my skin.

Eaglet! Horror floods me. *Eaglet!*

There are coughs. They all stand around me. Pavlik, Yulia, Anton, mama, Sonya with Lenochka, and grandma. Even Sim has come, wrapped in his usual lavish scarf. But no Lyosha Kabansky.

I'm suddenly livid.

Is your dick is still hurting? Good. I hope it does. I hope it burns like a skinned puppy dipped in pure surgical spirit.

They study me, their eyes questioning.

Eaglet! Are you alive?

No air enters my lungs.

Eaglet...

They shuffle closer, about to foist me their unsolicited mercy. As if it will help. Nothing can revive my boy. I have destroyed him, as I always wanted to.

Go away! Leave me alone! I want to die.

I turn to the wall.

Someone sits me up. I'm too weak to fight. I blink at the lights and the cheap curtains with flowers that resemble dead spiders and the figures around me.

Pavlik gives me a gentle squeeze. He has lost weight. His face is pallid, bluish almost, and his posture is somehow broken.

"Hey," he says.

I've been waiting to see him for so long that I don't know why I feel nothing. I want to be with him, and I don't. It's been two months, but it feels like two years. I don't sense him anymore, don't recognize him.

"How are you?"

I look at the floor.

"I got out last week." He takes my hand. "Are you ready to go home?"

I don't have a home. I have nothing.

"Irina, please."

I hear Yulia and Anton talking quietly, and mama and my auntie Sonya. They all stare at me as if I'm a ghost or an apparition, mama especially, and I can't bear it anymore, this pretense. I reach under the pillow and take out a notebook and a pencil one of the nurses gave me and write.

"I can't lie anymore, Pavlik."

He frowns. "What do you mean?"

I cradle my belly. "I'm sorry. I'm going to tell them—"

His eyes widen. "What? No." He stops my hand and whispers. "After the wedding. Please. I've been thinking this over."

"There will be no wedding." The pencil doesn't want to behave and slips out of my fingers. I grip it harder. "Don't worry. You won't have to endure me much longer."

"What are you talking about?"

I turn to a new page, clean and virgin.

Can you hold this? Can you hold this filth, paper?

"Lyosha Kabansky raped me every night for a year. The baby is his. He doesn't know it. I ran away from home to escape him."

The page shrinks under my words.

I destroyed you, eaglet. For this I will destroy myself.

209

CHAPTER TWENTY-FOUR

I get off the bed, tear out the page, and hold it in front of mama.

CHAPTER TWENTY-FIVE

SPIDER

I wait for mama to finish reading my note, then thrust it at Yulia. Here, read this. I force it on them, one by one. Know this. This is what happened. This, I want to scream. Do you believe me? You don't believe me? I don't give a shit if you believe me or not. Not anymore. They gape at me, shocked, confounded. Their expressions range from doubtful to reproachful to plain mean.

Hypocrites. It's not me who's crazy. You are. Look at you, pests in a circus. Animals. Cowards.

Mama makes a strange noise. The fake joy mask she has plastered over her face peels off and from underneath it emerges a slimy catfish, not quite drunk and not quite sober. She fixes me with a jealous stare.

"I knew it, I just knew it. Every night, huh? For a whole

year? I tell you what, daughter. If the bitch doesn't want it, the dog won't jump."

The boar, Mama. You mean, the boar. The boar will jump whether you want it to or not.

Her face contorts with hatred. "Who taught you this, huh?"

A lump rises in my throat.

Dua, says the eaglet.

Eaglet! My legs buckle.

Dua.

Eaglet, I thought—

Dua.

Stop. Please, stop!

Dua, dua, dua!

"*Dura,*" says mama with relish. She stares at me with that familiar glee that comes right before a beating. "I'll show you how to whore yourself with my man. I'll show you." She raises her arm. Flabby flesh hangs off it. I can see it through her maroon blouse, maroon like those wretched curtains.

I push her and bolt out of the room.

In the corridor I collide with a nurse, stumble, pick myself up, and force myself to keep moving. I'm dizzy. My legs tremble. I hold on to the wall and hobble along the hallway and stagger into the elevator. People look at me funny, ask me what's wrong. I pretend I don't hear them. At the bottom floor, I get out and cross the vestibule and push through the doors and step into the melting snow of the parking lot.

My belly cramps.

I grab on to a short, scraggly rowan tree. It grows on a patch of dirt. Clumps of last year's berries brush my face, shriveled and blackened. I pluck one and bite into it. It's dry like a bone and bitter, and it calms me. I eat a few more. Chew, swallow. They taste like dust. I watch my breath curl in the morning air and smell spring and take in a lungful.

Eaglet?

Silence.

Eaglet, please.

Faint movement.

Relief floods me. I clutch the rowan tree trunk, afraid I might fall.

I thought you died in me.

I didn't, says the eaglet.

I thought I destroyed you. I lower my head on my arm and feel hot water roll and drip and I let it. *You don't think I want you?*

Would you?

I'm sorry.

I breathe in and out and wipe my face.

Why did you do this?

To scare you, says the eaglet. *To make you remember.*

You did. You scared me to death. Please don't do this again.

I won't, if you hold your promise.

"Irina!" Pavlik runs across the lot, his face flushed.

I clasp the tree tighter.

"Why?" He's upon me, mad, like I've never seen him before. "Why did you tell them? Why couldn't you wait? Just one more month, Irina! Was it so hard to do?"

I avert my eyes.

He tugs on his hair and deflates. "I'm sorry."

I don't look up.

"Please, forgive me. I didn't mean it like that. I...I don't know why I said it."

I hear his breathing.

"Your doctor told us that that they found you on the roof last night. He said you wanted to jump. Is that true?"

I shrug.

"Oh, please, don't." He uncurls my fingers one by one and peels my hand off the tree. "I'm begging you, don't do it. He's not worth it. None of them are. Listen, I'm sorry I got mad. I understand why you did it. It's just that..."

A Zhiguli trundles by. Slush slopes over the curb.

He cups my belly. "Promise me, you won't leave me."

Liar. I push him away. *You wanted your papa to think you're straight and now I've ruined it.* I look up at his face, in his dark frightened eyes. *Why do you want a girl with a bastard baby? Give me one valid reason, and I will believe you.*

He answers, as if he heard my question. "You're like family to me, Irina. The family I've never had."

Family. I smirk. *Until you meet a boy who looks like Kostya, and fucks like Kostya. No, thanks. I'll be fine on my own.*

I pick the lint off his wool coat, and I study his mussed hair and his lips and soft face. Still young and yet old somehow, as if something has been cut from it. Something broke.

"I don't have to pretend when I'm with you, you know, don't have to hide or anything, I can just be myself."

You can with Sim.

"Even with Sim I'm acting like somebody else."

I touch his cheek slightly and I cup it and press my palm to his face. *Maybe it's time you stopped, then. Maybe it's time you stopped hiding.*

I hear footsteps.

Yulia and Anton walk over to us hand in hand and halt. Anton marches up to me and throws words in my face, measured and quiet. "I want you out of my son's life." Then he adds one more, loudly. "Out!"

I recoil.

"Papa, what's this about?"

"What? You know perfectly well what. I'm pulling you out of this crap you got yourself into, Pavlusha."

"We are pulling you out." Yulia's gaze stings me.

"Oh, I see. You two have decided on this behind my back, didn't you?" says Pavlik. "For my wellbeing, for my brilliant future. I'm sorry if I seem insensitive in any way, but can I ask you something, Papa? Did it ever occur to you, to consider," he says, and raises his voice, "or at least to pretend like you have considered my feelings on this matter?"

Anton wants to retort.

"No." Pavlik puts up his hand. "Please, hear me out. I'm tired. Tired of asking for approval from you, for my every step, for my every life decision. Do you think—"

"Approval? What right have you to talk about approval!" Anton shakes, Yulia strokes his arm. "You brought home this stray girl. And what did we do? Tell me. What did we do? We took her in."

Stray is right.

"We fed her, we clothed her. We thought you were in love, young reckless love. It's understandable, it happens. We forgave you. We thought you were going to be a young father. Your mother convinced your grandmother to move in with us, so that you two could have an apartment to start your own little family. I have lost my car as a result of this! And you...you lied to us."

The whine of an ambulance deafens me. A white van with red stripes rides past the parking lot. The guard salutes the driver from the booth by the fence, the gate slowly opens, and the van merges with the traffic. The whine grows weaker and dies.

"You know something, Papa," says Pavlik quietly, "this will blow your mind." He takes my hand and squeezes it. "I'm gay."

I stare at him.

His features turn sharp and insectile, contorted with fury

held back, deep under his face.

Wind cuts through my hospital bathrobe. My slippers are wet and cold from the moisture in the ground and I shiver.

"You what?" says Anton.

"What are you saying this nonsense for, Pavlusha?" says Yulia.

"What for?" Pavlik cracks up. "Mama, what do you mean, what for? Because I am. Haven't you noticed? You've read those notes, didn't you? Haven't you ever wondered?"

Tires rustle. Sim's car rolls up. The passenger window sinks down. "There you are." He looks us over. "This is hardly a convenient place for a talk. Irina, my child, you look frozen. Are they chilling you on purpose?"

He parks by the curb and prances out. "Why the long faces? Yulia Ibragimovna, my dear. Get off this dirty lawn, I implore you. You will mar your shoes."

"Oh," says Yulia, glancing down.

"Anton Borisovich!" He touches his shoulder, firmly, commandingly. "And here I thought you left without me. Tell me, have you picked out the venue yet? I happen to know a few excellent chefs, all very good friends of mine. From the most prestigious Moscow restaurants. Do you need me to put in a word?"

"Restaurants?"

"Yes, restaurants. For the wedding."

"There will be no wedding," says Anton flatly.

"Why not?" asks Sim, surprised. It's a well-played act. "It'd be easier for Pavel to get an international visa when he's married."

"A visa?" says Pavlik.

"We're going on tour." Sim grins. "To America."

To America? With me?

"To America?"

"New York, to be precise. If you leave something of value at home, like a wife and a new baby, for example, they'll know you won't defect, and you'll get your visa in no time."

Oh, and I'm a convenient tool to make it happen? I tear my hand out of Pavlik's.

"Well," Sim says to Pavlik's parents, "I think it's a good idea for your son to leave Moscow for a while, in light of recent events. Wouldn't you agree?"

Anton's face works on processing the information.

"This is very unexpected." Yulia is stone, only her lips move. "We need to discuss this, before making any decisions."

"Sim, thank you very much for the opportunity," says Pavlik, "but I'm not going anywhere."

I gape at him. *Have you lost your mind? Get out of this hole. Go.*

"This is no place to talk," says Sim. "Why don't we continue in the comfort of home? What do you say, Irina?"

I don't need to be asked twice. I hop in the car, into its soft, warm leather interior. I blow on my hands and rub them. Pavlik sits next to me. Sim gets in and calls out the window, "Meet you at your place!"

We take off.

"What did you say to them, you hooligan?" Sim says, watching us from the rearview mirror. "They look like they're about to pass out."

"I told them I'm gay," says Pavlik simply.

"What!" Sim gasps. "Did you, really?"

"Yes."

"Well, about time, my child, about time. Did you hear that, Irina? Listen to him. Lis-ten. He told them, just like that, under a rowan tree. How very romantic. Congratulations."

"You say it like it's no big deal."

"As it shouldn't be. It shouldn't be a big deal."

Sim is suddenly serious. "I'm sorry for what happened to you, Irina."

"Sim, can we please—"

"No, we cannot. Shut your precious hole. Irina, look at me."

I watch his eyes dance in the mirror.

"Your mother—I hope you don't mind me saying this, but—what a fish, that woman. What a fish!"

A catfish, to be precise. I smile. *And I don't mind at all.*

"You've grown wings, my child. Good for you. Good for you for exposing the truth."

And these words he says, they take the weight off my chest.

Good for you. Good for you.

I feel light, so light. Validated.

You salacious lump of fat, Sim. You're the one who's abusing Pavlik, and I loathe you for it, but thank you.

"Can we please not talk about this right now? I don't think—"

"Quiet! I'm talking to your future wife. That nasty pig. What's he got for a cock, a pizzle?"

"Sim, please!"

"Don't interrupt me!"

I grin. *A pizzle. Yeah, something like that.*

Pavlik turns to me. "You know, sometimes I can't help it but to experience both extreme love and extreme hatred toward this man."

I'm beginning to understand you.

"Liar. You worship me. Tell me I'm wrong."

"Oh, but how can I?"

We stop at the light.

Sim lights a cigarette. "You don't mind if I smoke?"

I shake my head.

"You can open the window, if you want."

I wind it down. One of the vending kiosks lining the street sells audiocassettes and it blasts Grebenshchikov's song about the golden city, an ox, a lion, and an eagle.

My skin expands. I want to drop it.

Pedestrians crawl across the street, sluggish and stiff, their bent bodies garbed in cheap furs. Rodents.

Food. You're nothing but food for me.

I flex my fingers. They feel strange, thinning, as if they're fanning out into feathers. My heart beats hard.

Eaglet, look at me. I'm the eagle from this song.

I see it, says the eaglet. *Can we go flying?*

I lean out and—

The hide of the mouse rips open and out bursts an eagle.

It climbs out of the car and spreads its wings and flaps them once and soars over Moscow, and it looks to the eagle far from golden. It's dull and monotonous and dirty with melting snow and crisscrossed with roads and train tracks and spiked with naked trees and stacked with dingy apartment blocks squatting in a colorless haze as if they're taking a dump. It's a living thing, Moscow, a web of concentric lines. It squirms and clamors and hungers, an insect with many legs projecting from its fat, busy center and its five red eyes in the middle, the Red Square. Spiral orbs wind around it. The Boulevard ring. The Garden ring. Six more.

It's a spider.

It sees the eagle and flexes. It wants to catch it and to liquefy it and to suck it dry and leave an empty husk. More of its red eyes open. Soviet flags of the rallies and demonstrations and protest. They stare at the eagle.

It screams and, distracted, slams into the wall of a Stalinist high-rise, one of the Seven Sisters, seven venom glands topped with sharp steeples, drops of clear toxin trembling on their tips. The eagle's feathers brush against the concrete and break off and seesaw to the ground.

The eagle tumbles down, recovers.

The spider gives an earsplitting squall. Car honks, car breaks, and animal shrieks. It gathers its legs. Its eyes swivel and focus on the bird and it jumps.

The eagle looks on in horror.

The whole of Moscow detaches itself from the ground. Its roots drip poison, years of famine, oppression, corruption. Slavery. Civil war. Collectivization, communism, socialism. Red Terror. It's the poison that intoxicates every creature born into it from their first scream; strangles it, squashes it, makes it crawl in misery and submit to its power until it has full control. Until it eradicates will, confidence, individuality. Until there is nothing left—no optimism, no faith—only spite. Bitter, furtive spite followed by depression, alcoholism, and suicide.

The spider's mass and enormity blackens the sky. For a moment, it hovers in the air and rushes down.

The eagle takes wing to the side, desperate to escape the shadow above, and that's when it sees the other birds, colorful and exotic parrots of all types. Cockatiels, popinjays, lories. Macaws. They squawk and dart and dive and dodge and scatter. The uproar is deafening.

The eagle sees a dot in their midst, a butterfly. A black admiral. It flitters in confusion. Then a strong wind hits them from above, a gust of grit, twigs, and dirt, followed by darkness. The eagle loses altitude, fights to stay aloft, tumbles, rights itself meters from the ground and sees the butterfly hovering above a dark shape looking up at the sky.

The boar.

Its eyes glisten. It watches the butterfly flit close and gulps it down. The eagle shrieks, rams into the boar, cuts it open with its talons, and that's when the spider crushes them both with its bulk.

I jerk. My heart pounds in my ears. I'm sitting in Sim's car. He's smoking outside.

"How are you feeling?" says Pavlik. "You slept through the ride."

I rub my face, trying to clear my head.

"You know, if not for you, I wouldn't have had the courage to tell them, maybe not for years. So thank you, thank you very much. I feel lighter somehow." He wants to tell me more, but I want to get out of the car, to feel it.

I open the door and step out onto the street.

Cold fear shoots up my spine.

A tremor runs through the cracked asphalt, a stealthy rumble. The city thrums under my feet, a living breathing spider, and I know it wants it to happen.

It wants the boar to kill the butterfly.

CHAPTER TWENTY-SIX

OTTER

I stand in front of the mirror in the ZAGS foyer. It's nine fifty a.m. on the third Saturday of March, the day of our marriage registration, Yulia's doing. She gave two bribes to get around my age and to push us ahead in the queue. I look at reflections of gaudy sofas, wall panels inlaid with nauseating depictions of spousal happiness, and other waiting couples. Their veils and suits and bouquets. Their friends' red sashes stamped with WITNESS in gold. And my tacky white dress. Grandma made it from a curtain, since none of the store gowns would fit me. Puffy sleeves, frilly skirt.

So much for an eagle, you dumb, gravid chicken.

"Nervous?" Pavlik fingers his necktie.

I push his hand away, smooth the knot, and tighten it.

Not really. I've been waiting for this moment for over a year now. I finger the knife wrapped in a hanky and stashed in my left sleeve.

"Me too." He sighs. "I just hope no one makes a scene. There's been enough drama this week, you know?" He inspects the tie in the mirror, brushes off invisible lint, and flattens his hair.

That's a good hope to have. My hope is to kill Lyosha before he kills you.

"I know what you're thinking."

I tilt my head. *Do you?*

"Put it out of your mind, please. Let's forget about everything for a day. It's our day, it's supposed to be happy. Look, we're surrounded with people. What could possibly go wrong?" He groans. "Stop staring at me like that."

A woman's voice rings out, "Pavel and Irina Baboch! Five minutes!"

Irina Baboch. Will it really happen?

"Pavlusha, it's almost time," calls Yulia.

"Just a moment! Irina," he says to me, "let's enjoy today, okay? Let's have fun."

Oh, I'll have fun. You'll see.

"I do love you, you know."

I back away.

"How else can I prove it to you, die for you or what?" He gives an uneasy chuckle.

My heart stills. *Don't say it. Don't fucking say it!*

"Do you love me?"

His face is so close.

Of course I do, you piece of glorious ass. Every bride has already checked you out at least twice and burned a hole in me with jealous stares. Go tell them you're gay so they'll stop hating me.

"You know something? I'm scared...scared of leaving you. I've gotten used to your constant presence, your silence. I can hear you thinking. You're always there, always listening. I'll miss you, Irina. I'll miss you very much." He plays with my fingers. "Will you miss me?"

I close my eyes. *Stop, please. I'm already bleeding.*

The front door bangs open.

Lenochka runs up to me first, grabs handfuls of my skirt. "Irkadura is getting married! Irkadura is getting married!"

"Shut your mouth," says Sonya. "Irka! You fat dolt."

"Oy! Irka! I can't believe it. You look so pretty!" Grandma claps her hands and cackles. Her golden teeth shine dully.

I cringe.

"My sweet daughter! Look at you." Mama is the last to greet me, already tipsy. I endure her wet kisses and weak embrace.

"Good morning, Marina Viktorovna," says Yulia. "So nice of you to come right on time."

"Yulia Davydovna!" Mama scoops her up. Yulia cringes.

"Forgive me, Marina Viktorovna"—Anton clears his throat and props up his glasses—"I don't mean to be rude in any way, so please, don't take this personally, but may I ask for a favor? Today is a special day for our children. I'd appreciate it if you went light on the alcohol."

"Huh? Why is this any of your business? It's my daughter's wedding. My daughter." She beats her chest. "I have the right to celebrate how I want—"

"Excuse me!" Pavlik waves his arms about. "Irina and I have a request for all of you. Please, be civil today. Just one day. Can you manage it for us? Mama, why are you looking at me like it's my funeral?"

"Funeral! That's funny. Dead groom! Dead groom!"

Lenochka hops.

Sonya smacks her.

"Pavlusha!" Yulia is shocked. "You must never say things like that. It's bad luck."

And I hear it. The tremor in the fabric of the city. A thump and a grunt and a gallop. The boar is on its way. I touch the knife through my sleeve. The handle sits at my elbow and the blade at my wrist.

Come closer, piggy, closer. I will gut you.

Our names are called again and we're ushered into the ceremony hall. It's stark, utilitarian, and empty, save for the threadbare rug leading to a massive desk with a couple of Russian flags on it and rows of chairs by the walls.

A dumpy woman dressed in a drab skirt suit stands at the desk. Short arms, bandy legs, clasped hands over her solid midline.

An over-fed otter suffering from boredom.

"The registry office of the city of Moscow greets you." Her tone is dull and she lisps a little.

You should work at a funeral home, you have the perfect intonation for it.

"Respected Pavel and Irina. Today is the day of your marriage. In this large and complex world you have found each other to become the most cherished people in each other's lives." Words fall out of her mouth like stones.

I tune out and listen for the boar.

After she's done with her monotonous rumble, she asks us if we want to marry.

"Yes," says Pavlik.

I nod.

She asks me again.

"What are you asking her for? She's mute." Mama hiccups.

"Slap her, scold her, it's no good. Believe me, I've tried everything. She's been like that since she was two."

I clench my fists. The knife tip punctures the skin on my wrist. I ignore it. My mind is still. My eyes are focused on mama's pasty, wasted face. A word rises in my throat and slams into the backs of my teeth. I roll it on my tongue.

Dura.

The otter woman recites the codex of marriage, asks for our signatures, and pronounces us husband and wife. We walk up to her desk. Pavlik pulls a velvet box from his pocket, takes out one of the two plain gold bands, and slips it on my right ring finger. I mechanically slip the other one on his.

He kisses me, a brief peck on the lips.

My mind is so far away, I barely sense it. The ground throbs in rhythm to the boar's gallop. It vibrates the soles of my feet and sends ripples across the floor and I notice the rug shift imperceptibly.

The March of Mendelssohn blares out of the sputtering speakers. Mama sobs loudly. Everyone claps and congratulates us.

Pavlik leads me out.

We descend ten steps down to a black shiny Chaika parked by the ZAGS porch and sink into the worn indented seats and wave, watching the crowd disperse into cars behind us.

We stop at the Moscow State University observation point at Sparrow Hills and take obligatory pictures with Pavlik throwing me on his arm and Pavlik pressing his lips to mine and Pavlik hugging me and even Pavlik trying to lift me up, per tradition, and giving up because I'm too heavy. After an hour of this, we climb back inside the Chaika and head for the city center to the restaurant.

I should be excited, but I merely glaze over the gilded letters on the porch gable, PRAGA, the merry faces and the sparkling eyes and the rich carpet and the marble and the lavish décor.

We halt in the doors to the dinner hall. The chef, a portly man in a white hat and a double-breasted jacket, greets us and hands us crystal flutes filled with champagne. I take mine and down it and strain to listen for any movement, glimpse the end of a long table covered with linen and plates and folded napkins and candleholders. Patterned hunter-green carpet on the floor. Garish light. The back wall is a panorama of Kremlin set behind marble columns.

We enter and I stumble and almost fall.

Pavlik catches my elbow. "Are you all right?"

Panic shoots through my veins. I'm back to being two, standing in the balcony room of our apartment. The windows are hung with maroon curtains. Same color, same thread.

Pavlik leads me to the head of the table and draws out a chair. "Irina, what is it?"

I'm fixated on the drapes, on the fabric, the way it hangs and folds. Everything else recedes into fog, the guests pulling out chairs and easing themselves in and chattering and picking up their drinks.

Anton uses his fork to make a tinkling sound on his glass. "May I ask for everyone's attention?"

They hush and look at him, expectant, about thirty festively decked out people—most of whom I don't know, some distant relatives and friends of Pavlik's family—but then I see Sim and Tanechka and a few other actors from the troupe whom I recognize, and Ilinichna, and everyone from my side except Lyosha Kabansky who was forbidden to show up, on Yulia's insistence, and was kept in the dark as to the whereabouts of the venue.

You've found out anyway, you swine. Haven't you?

227

"Today is a big day for us," says Anton. "Thank you all for gathering here to celebrate the joining of our two families, and the creation of a brand new family."

Pavlik whispers to me, "You okay?"

I force a smile.

Anton takes off his glasses, cleans them on a napkin, and props them back on. "Pavlusha, our dear Pavlusha, our only son, our pride, our joy"—his chin jitters—"we give you in the hands of this young beautiful woman, Irina."

"That's right," says mama. Grandma shushes her.

"Irina, Pavel." Anton puffs up, like an inflated owl. "We hope you take care of each other until the end of your days."

Until the end of our days. I touch the knife.

"We wish you love, health, and prosperity. May...your child have loving parents. To the newlyweds!" He raises his glass.

Voices join him.

"To the newlyweds!"

"Bitter!"

"Oy! Bitter, how bitter!"

I'm suddenly petrified. I've been waiting for this for so long that I've forgotten I want it.

Pavlik helps me up. "Is it okay if I...kiss you for real this time?" He looks at me strangely.

I shake my head. *You don't have to. You can just twist me out of the way and they won't see. I must disgust you, I know. You probably—*

He cups my face and he's kissing me. At first I try to breathe and then I can't. There is no air, only the warm and soft feeling of his lips and his taste and water in my eyes that spills and rolls down my cheeks and I'm mad at myself for kissing him back, mad for losing it and for loving it and for wanting more.

Someone begins to count.

"One, two, three…"

"I want to," slurs mama, "say something."

We pull apart, flushed, surprised. Blood pounds in my head and my heart beats so hard it hurts. I grip the edge of the table to stop my hands from shaking.

Mama labors up. She can barely stand upright, a wavering finger directed at me. "Look at you. I carried you right here"— she slaps under her breasts—"just like you're carrying your brat right now."

Oh no, Mama. Don't.

"Irka, I'm proud of you, but you need to understand something." She burps. "I'm still angry with you. That baby has no right to be. No right!"

The room goes still.

"Sit!" Grandma tugs on her arm.

"Let go of me. You spoke your mind at my wedding. Now it's my turn."

And I see myself and mama, only one generation down. Same intolerance, control, and preachy tone.

"Pavel, what a handsome young man you are." Mama's voice quivers. "An actor. You have good parents, good genes. You'll have a good future. And my Irka…"

Please don't.

"She's not a match for you. You're making a big mistake." Mama surveys the table. "You all think the same, don't you? You," she says, and stabs a finger at Yulia, "you're an educated woman. Why don't you say anything, huh? Your son doesn't want to be with my daughter, you know that! Your son—"

Grandma yanks her down and slaps her.

Mama gasps, holds her cheek.

"Marina Viktorovna," says Yulia through a smile, "why do you say such things at your daughter's wedding? I'm not sure I understand—"

"She's a dura, that's why," says grandma.

"That's absolutely not true, Marina Viktorovna." Pavlik cuts through the muttering. "I very much want to be with Irina and I apologize if I have made such an unfavorable impression on you. This is entirely my fault."

A shadow passes by the window and I jump.

It's here. It found us.

The boar.

CHAPTER TWENTY-SEVEN

CATFISH

I doubted myself again. I was right all along. I grab Pavlik's arm. *You need to leave! Now!* I pull him away from the table and I want to tell him what's about to happen; instead, I screech in short urging bursts. *Curse my tongue. Rip it out, please, I don't want it. It's useless!* I bite on it. Warm blood fills my mouth. *If I could only talk to you, if I could only explain—*

"Hey, where are you—" He reads the terror in my eyes. "Is Lyosha here?"

I nod.

"I thought he might show up. Please, Irina, calm down. There is nothing he can do. Look, we're in a room full of people."

I hang on his arm.

The doors burst open.

"Surprise!" Lyosha is pissed, pissed good. Unshaven, unwashed, in a crumpled jacket and stained trainers, with red carnations in one hand and a bottle of Stolichnaya in the other. He grins a stupid smile. "Holy gee, Irkadura. What a dress. That's one helluva dress. Blast me, you're big. Look at you, about to pop, aren't you?"

Heads turn.

I let go of Pavlik's arm, hide my hands behind my back, pinch the tip of the knife and tug on it, pulling it out.

"You thought I wouldn't come, didn't you?" Lyosha waddles to the table. "Marinka, you dumb bitch. Why didn't you tell me you'd be in Praga? Why did you tell me to go to that Georgian pigsty?"

Mama shrinks into the chair.

"Ah, no matter." He dismisses her with the wave of a hand. "I've found you, didn't I? I have good friends." He stares at me.

The ravens.

"Thought I'd see my daughter off myself."

The blade sits in my palm now, new and sharp. I picked the small carving knife from our wedding presents for its length. It fit perfectly against my forearm. I hide it in the folds of my skirt and the handle gets stuck at the cuff. I unwrap the hanky, all the while glaring at Lyosha.

Remember you asked me where I was going? Well, this is the place. They butcher boars here, gut them, roast them, and serve them on a platter, their asses stuffed with lard.

He sneers at me.

You know what they do to make the boars taste better? They kick them for days—so they get tender and juicy—and then they rip out their dicks, just to hear them squeal.

"Aleksey Ivanovich!" Anton stands. "You're not supposed

to be here."

"Well, I am here, aren't I?" Lyosha plods over.

Closer, come closer.

There are four chairs between us, the farthest two occupied by two guests, the closest two by Yulia and Anton.

Pavlik notices the knife.

"What are you...put it away!"

I sidestep him.

You're drunk out of your mind, Lyosha, which is good. It will make my job easier.

"Irina!" Pavlik reaches for my hand.

I dodge him.

"Excuse me, Aleksey Ivanovich, but both Irina and I would like for you to leave," says Pavlik. "Immediately."

"What?" Lyosha halts next to Yulia.

"Pavlusha, son, sit down. Let me handle this."

"No, Papa. Allow me. It's my wedding, after all." Pavlik strides to my side, his eyes on Lyosha. "I thought I told you in plain Russian. We'd like for you to leave. You're not welcome here. Do you understand?"

Comprehension wrinkles Lyosha's porcine face. "Who says? Irka? Ha! She can't talk. How do you know what she wants? My Irka wants to see me, don't you?"

I want to see you dead.

His face darkens. "You do, don't you?"

"No, she doesn't." Pavlik makes another swipe at me.

I edge away, work at the cuff, free the knife handle, and grasp it.

"I heard that husband prick of yours is not the father of your brat." He stops, blocked by Anton. "I say, ditch the faggot. Come home. We'll raise him the right way, like a proper man, proper Russian, not some stinking Jew."

233

CHAPTER TWENTY-SEVEN

"Lyosha—" starts mama.

"Shut your mouth, slut!"

You couldn't guess it on your own, could you? You had to wait for the ravens to tell you. Did they drive you here, too? Words choke me. I want to scream them at his face. A droplet of sweat runs down my nose and I sense it hanging on the very tip, and grip the knife harder.

"Aleksey Ivanovich." Pavlik shakes. "I'm asking you one last time. We request that you leave at once, or we'll have to call militia."

"Pavlusha, Aleksey Ivanovich, let's take it easy." Anton tries to placate. "Let's all—"

"Papa, we don't want him here!"

Not a scrape of a fork, not a breath.

"Did you know your son is a homo? Did you?" Lyosha seizes a fistful of the tablecloth and yanks at it. Glasses fall, plates clatter together.

Lenochka shrieks, Sonya scolds her.

Yulia hangs over Lyosha, hissing. "Get out of here, you damned alcoholic."

Pavlik sucks in air.

"You think it's him who knocked her up?" Lyosha roars with laughter. "How do you think he did it?" He turns to Pavlik. "Show me your cock, I want to see it."

Pavlik stares. His cheeks sprout red blotches.

"What, you haven't got one, have you? Here is a bit of news for you, for your wedding night. It was I who fucked her." His blood-shot eyes bulge. "And I'm not the first, you hear? You know how many were before me? She's lain with all of Marinka's mongrels, every one of them. She's a whore. That's whom you married. A whore!"

"My wife...is not...a whore," says Pavlik.

He takes two steps to Lyosha, raises a fist, and drives it into his jaw. Lyosha sways off balances for a moment and drops to the floor with a thud. The vodka bottle breaks and soaks the carpet and the red carnations scatter. Mama screams. People jump up and crane their necks.

"Damned faggot." Lyosha scrambles up, the jagged bottleneck in front of him.

The eaglet kicks me. *Get it! Get it!*

I will. And I charge.

"Irina!" Pavlik grabs for me, misses, steps on my skirt. It rips. I stumble. Lyosha ogles the knife in my hand. His eyes widen. He stoops and aims the broken bottle at my belly. I'm falling straight toward it. There is nothing for me to hold on to.

A body rams into my side.

I yelp and topple to the floor, the knife clutched firmly in my hand.

Pavlik is in my place, his arms spread wide, the black sleeves of his wedding jacket like the black wings of a butterfly. Lyosha's hand moves upward. The glass teeth cut into Pavlik's neck, that tender place between the shirt collar and his cleanly shaved chin. Blood splutters on the knot, the tie knot that I smoothed and tightened just this morning.

Pavlik draws in air.

For a second they regard each other, then they tip over and drop, Lyosha flat on his back, Pavlik on top of him.

The hall goes deathly quiet.

I blink, focus. Table legs, chairs, shoes. Pavlik convulses, and blood bubbles from the cut in his neck, staining Lyosha's jacket. Lyosha swears and shoves him off. Pavlik flops to the floor, face up.

My mind leaves me.

I scream, get up on all fours, and leap at Lyosha. He's so

surprised, he doesn't resist me. I straddle him, belly to belly, lift my arm, and plunge the blade deep into his gut. The knife becomes one thing with my hand, the razor-sharp talon of an eagle. I wrench it out and stab him again. And again. And again.

Lyosha's arms fly up, then drop. He gurgles.

My hand gets slippery, sticky. I taste salt on my lips. The blood stains my dress red, red like the Soviet flag, like the pioneer neckerchiefs I used to wear to school, like the spots on my sheets after I was taken, like the ragged hole in Kostya's chest, like the eyes of the spider.

Like the scattered red carnations.

Do it! Do it! The eaglet pokes and jabs and kicks.

I am, eaglet. I am.

Gut it!

I am gutting it.

Cut off its dick!

I will!

There are screams all around me. Someone lifts me by the armpits. I toss my head up and holler with the force of years of silence. I howl and wail until my voice cracks, until I grow short of breath, and then I see her in front of me.

Mama.

"Lyosha, my Lyosha...what did she do to you? What did the dura do to you?" She shakes his limp body. Her upper lip curls, her thin mustache bristles. Her dazed eyes fix on me. "You bitch." She looks scary and ghastly, some of her teeth missing, her hair lank over her face. "You killed him, Irkadura. You killed him!" She lifts her hand and—

I'm two. Today I've learned how to say my first word. I've been poking mama and I woke her up and I've been telling her this new word I've learned, this word she always calls me, but for some reason mama is unhappy. She's mad. She screams at me.

"Irka, who taught you this, huh? You dumb girl. Her hand flies up. "I'll show you——"

I drop the knife and block her arm. The word I held inside me for fourteen years breaks through.

"Dura," I say. I can roll the *r*. It feels awkward, moving my tongue, forming sounds. I try again. "Dura."

"What?" Mama's eyes round.

"Dura," I repeat, sucking in air. "Dura, dura, dura!"

Mama's face scrunches up, as if she's about to cry.

There is chaos in the room, frantic shouts.

"Call the ambulance! Quick!"

"He's hurt!"

Someone hauls me off Lyosha. I wrest out of the hold, drop to my knees, and push Yulia out of the way.

"Pavlik," I say, for the first time. I touch his face and search his eyes, trying to see something in them, anything.

There is nothing.

They're still.

He's gone.

CHAPTER TWENTY-EIGHT

VOBLA

Warm fluid trickles down my legs, wets my stockings, more of it gushes out and drenches my skirt. At first I think it's piss, then I remember that it must be my waters. Sim and Tanechka drag me away from Pavlik's body and prop me against the wall. My stained bridal pumps slide off my swollen feet. My hands shake, my breath rattles. Noises whirr in my ears, wails, cries, echoes of militia and ambulance sirens in the street, getting closer. A tight hot belt cinches my belly.

I double over. *Eaglet...*

It's time.

Why?

I'm not hungry anymore.

But it's early.

You're the one who did it.

I cradle my belly. *I did what? Let the animal out?*

Yes. Now let me out all the way.

Stay! They'll take you away from me.

What for?

I killed a man.

No, says the eaglet. *You slaughtered a boar, like you promised you would.*

"She's all wet," says Sim.

Tanechka feels under my skirt. "Her waters broke."

He killed Pavlik, eaglet. He killed him.

"It," says the eaglet. *"It" killed Pavlik. You slaughtered "it" because "it" deserved it.*

But it's my fault, eaglet. My fault.

No.

"Tell the medics she's in labor!"

I'll go to jail.

"Breathe, Irina, breathe."

Eagles don't go to jail, people do.

"Are you listening? Listen to me. I need you to breathe. In, out. In, out."

What do eagles do?

"Yuri Grachev, ambulance doctor. What happened?"

"She's in labor."

Cold fingers lift my face, pull open my eyelids. A swarthy man with close-set beady eyes swims into focus. He smells of disinfectant and onions. Behind him I see grandma and Sonya and Lenochka, hands to their mouths.

Eagles fly.

Where?

Away.

I don't want to fly away without you. You're the only one I have left. I've lost everyone else.

I'll come with you.

You will?

Yes, I will. Mama.

Two medics frisk about my dress, and haul me onto a stretcher.

"Pavlik!" Hands push me down.

I want to sit up again and I can't. Another contraction, stronger this time, circles me in flames. I groan and pull up my knees and hug them and close my eyes.

"You'll be fine, Irina," Sim whispers in my ear. "You're stronger than you think you are. You have wings now. Use them, before they clip them." A pat on the shoulder, and he's gone.

I'm hoisted into the van.

One of the medics climbs in after me. She's a middle-aged woman, a goose stupefied from fatigue, her thin lips smeared with faded lipstick, her cheeks sunken, her gaze dim. She drags a scuffed metal case from under a bench, unlocks it, takes out a gauzy cloth, and starts wiping my face without a word.

A young militiaman in an ill-fitting uniform, dry as a vobla, bangs the doors shut and sits next to the medic.

The engine revs, the ambulance jolts, and the siren whoops with annoying repetition.

My head rocks from side to side.

The pain is too much. All I want to do is to stop existing somehow, to stop seeing Pavlik's face and his dead eyes; instead, a boiling flood rises from my gut and slips into my mouth. Words. Words I haven't spoken yet. The tangle of them presses forth. I look at the medic and at the militant.

"I can talk now." It comes out clumsy. I moisten my lips, and I want to laugh and to cry at the same time.

"Shhh," says the medic. "We'll be there soon."

"How far?" says the militant.

"Fifteen minutes or so. What will you do with her?"

"Nothing yet. Think for yourself, all right. First she's got to deliver her baby, yes? After that, I'll hand her over to the branch she's registered with, and then it's out of my hands. They'll take her to court, I imagine, or, who knows. Maybe they'll put her in a nuthouse."

"She knifed both of them?"

"No, just her father. That other one—"

"Her own father?" She shoots me a look of horror.

"It was not my father," I say. "It was a boar."

The militant whispers something to the medic. She nods, her enlarged eyes on me, a hand over her mouth.

"I couldn't talk for fourteen years," I say. Rolling the *r* gives me the best pleasure. I want to talk and talk and talk. I want somebody to hear me.

The woman only shakes her head.

"The catfish..." I catch my breath. Talking is hard work. "...thought I was a weak little mouse. It took away my voice and it swallowed me, but I got stuck in its throat. I used everything I had, my teeth, my claws, and I wouldn't go down."

"Ruslan!" she tells the driver. "Hurry up. The patient is delirious."

"So it spit me out," I tell the militant.

He slides the visor cap on his eyes and pretends to nap.

"Five more blocks!" says Ruslan's cheery voice from behind the partition window.

"Then it saw that I'm not a mouse anymore. They all saw it, all the beasts. They saw that I'm an eagle and that I have a voice."

The woman doesn't look at me. She's taking notes.

"I let the animal out of me, that's all I did. Is it a crime to want to talk?"

I get no answer, only the engine rumble and the monotone whine of the siren.

"It doesn't matter that I can talk now, does it? You don't hear me."

A contraction forces me to roll to the side and I crouch and pant. When it passes, I sit up on my elbows and I see their indifference and their apathy and their pretense and I get mad.

"You know who you are?" I tell the medic.

She looks up.

"You're a dumb goose. You're so afraid, you forgot you're afraid. Fear has soaked into your muscles and made you insensitive. You pretend like you don't care, that's your escape. Torpor, stupidity, and cowardice."

She flinches. "What?"

"Don't listen to her." The militant yawns and puts on his cap. "She's schizo."

"And you," I say, and rivet my eyes on him, "are a vobla. A brainless, spineless fish without teeth. You feed on rotting gruel, on silt and on mud. That's your diet. You're a cheat and you live off bribes."

He goes pale. "You shut your mouth! What did I tell you? She's schizo."

The driver honks and curses.

The van lurches.

"You know I'm right," I say. "Both of you. You're so used to hypocrisy, you simply don't see it anymore. It's a nice way to exist, but a terrible way to live. You're nothing but empty husks. You fell into the trap of trusting this place, its lies, its propaganda, and you've lost your humanness as a result. It's been sucked out of you, but you don't miss it, do you? What's to miss? Honesty? Kindness? Compassion? No, fuck it. It's too painful, too hard, it's easier to be a dimwitted beast."

The siren dies.

The van stops, the doors open, and the fresh scent of rain wafts in. The medic and the militant get out. A grim hospital attendant hoists out the stretcher and heaves me onto the gurney.

"Oho! A bride? What's all this blood?"

"I practiced in butchery today, for the first time," I say. It gives me immense satisfaction to move my tongue, to make sounds, to hear them ring out. "I gutted a boar. I can practice on you, if you'd like."

He recoils. "Crazy, this one."

"Do you want her to give birth right here, in the street? Roll her in!"

I bend from a spasm. Light rain speckles my face. The gurney jiggles over cracks in the asphalt and jolts over the curb and then it's smooth. I'm in the clinic lobby and all around me is a sharp medicinal smell and harsh lights and impartial faces.

"What's this?" says one of the nurses. "Good God, look at all the blood!"

"She murdered her father at her wedding. Hard to imagine, yes?" The militant shakes his head. "Knifed him in broad daylight. He died right on the spot, the poor fellow."

"You don't say. Why did you bring her here?"

"What are you, blind? She's in labor. Speed it up somehow, will you? I know you can do it. I've got to watch her so she won't run off or do something funny, and I want to be home by dinner."

I force myself to sit up. My wet bangs fall on my eyes and I brush them off. "Don't worry," I say. "I'm not going anywhere. Go home and eat your gruel, you fucking vobla."

"What did you call me?"

"Fucking vobla."

He rushes at me and, for a moment, we glare at each other. "You're lucky I don't hit pregnant women."

"You're lucky I don't have a knife."

The din of the lobby dies. The staff behind the registration window, a doctor passing with a stack of papers, pregnant women and their relatives seated in chairs along the wall, they all stare me up and down.

"What is it, you don't like my dress?"

I look at myself and laugh. My gown is torn, stained, and wet. From under its hem stick out my dirty feet in ripped nylon tights. Red gloves of Lyosha's gore cover my hands. And the odor I emit, the stink of sweat and blood and vaginal fluids, is revolting.

The nurse and the militant wheel me into the elevator. We ride five floors up and they roll me out into a corridor faced with pale blue ceramic tiles.

A powerful cramp seizes me and I shriek.

"Keep your mouth shut!" says the militant.

They thrust me into a long narrow room already packed with ten or so women. Cows, vulnerable and exhausted, left to struggle by themselves.

"Go wash yourself." The nurse hands me a hospital gown. "The bathroom is at the end of the hallway. Come on, she's in no state to go anywhere," she tells the militant. "Go have tea in the canteen. This is no place for men."

"No funny business, understand? I'll find you if you run." He gives me a dubious look and departs.

The women study me silently.

I wriggle out of the wretched dress, tear off the tights, the bra, and the panties, and toss them onto the floor.

"What's happened to you?" says a girl from the bed by the

window. She clutches her bulging sides and rocks a little.

"My mama's boyfriend raped me and got me pregnant," I say with surprising calm.

"No. The blood."

"I killed him."

She gapes in horror. They all do, shrinking back.

I press the robe to my breasts and stagger out.

CHAPTER TWENTY-NINE

EAGLE

After nine agonizing hours of contractions, I'm hauled into the delivery room. My pubes get shaved with a rusty razor. An enema is forced in my anus. The doctor, a brusque woman with coarse canine features, declares that I'm unable to dilate. Bluish light reflects in the lines of her face, her silhouette stark against the tiled walls.

"Five centimeters," she says, and wags her head. "You're not trying hard enough."

The baby's head is ripping me. The pain is unbearable. Wet with sweat, feverish and frantic, I scream.

"What are you yelling for?" The doctor rounds on me. "Who asked you to get pregnant? It didn't hurt screwing, did it? But now you cry like it hurts? Shut your mouth and push!" Her harsh face twists with resentment.

"What would you know about screwing?" I say. "When was the last time you got laid, you sadistic bitch? Who'd want to fuck you? You're nothing but a yapping mutt—" Pain cuts me off.

"Push, dura, push!"

I grunt and pant and squeeze.

"Bad mother! You'll suffocate the baby! Push!"

Two nurses throw themselves on my stomach and press down.

I can't draw air.

"Give me the scalpel. I'm cutting her open." The doctor leans in and hot fire splits my groin.

I holler in agony.

"I got the head! Push!"

I push and feel something huge slide out of me. My belly collapses on itself like a deflated balloon.

"It's a boy!" the nurse says.

"Pavlik." I can't see through my tears. "Pavlik!"

I hear a cry, feeble at first. With each breath it grows stronger. Then I see him. A reddish squirmy baby boy held in gloved hands. The nurse ties a tag with a number to his foot and an identical one to my wrist.

"Give him to me." My voice is hoarse from screaming.

The nurse wipes him, swaddles him, and carries him out.

"Where is she taking him? I want my baby! Give me my baby!"

My abdomen contracts and something else plops out. I'm so weak, I can barely move. The nurse cleans me roughly and begins stitching me up, sticking the needle right into my flesh.

And I lose it.

I wake up in a dark room. My head spins. My breasts ache, engorged with milk. There is no baby at my side. I throw off the blanket and shift my legs and stifle a cry. My crotch ripples with pain. I grip the headboard, struggle to standing, and listen.

Soft snores. Measured breathing. Bodies around me on beds. Gray light seeps in from the gap in the drapes and I glimpse a sliver of the sky hung with clouds.

"That's where the golden city is," I whisper, "above the clouds. The place where eagles live."

I step into the slippers, creep to the door, and crack it open. The hinges screech. I freeze. Someone rolls over with a sigh. I wait until the bed springs settle and slip out, shuffling toward the babies' cries. I can hear them coming from the corridor ahead. I pass by the nurses' station where a nurse sleeps with her head on the desk, turn to the right, and come upon a line of square windows.

The nursery.

I press my face to the glass.

Weak light illuminates two rows of insect-like trolleys on casters. Atop each of them is a plastic tray with a newborn, about twenty total, swaddled head to toe, tags with numbers tied around their bottom ends. Most of them are asleep, a few are crying. Their tiny scrunched up faces gape with toothless holes.

"Pavlik." My breath fogs up the glass.

I try the door. It's unlocked. I step in.

"Pavlik?"

The voice that comes from the corner of the room, from the trolley by the plastic baby scales, stops crying. I walk up to it and lean over.

A face looks at me, round and stubborn, like mine. Eyebrows in a frown. Eyes dark, unblinking. Beads of tears on the eyelashes.

I check the tag. "Baboch Pavel Pavlovich, boy, labor: March twentieth, three twenty a.m. Weight three kilograms, height fifty centimeters." My hands shake so hard, it takes me several attempts to lift him out and to free my breast.

He latches on at once.

My nipples buzz. Milk drips from my other breast in a warm trickle and soaks the robe. I stroke his cheek, his forehead, his nose. I feel my tears dampen his blanket. "Pavlik, it's Mama. How are you?"

He breathes quietly, working. His nostrils flare.

"It's me, remember? Is it okay if I call you Pavlik?"

Footsteps echo from the corridor.

My heart skips a beat.

Pavlik spits the nipple out and hiccups. A thin line of saliva trails from his puckered lips.

"I won't let them take you away." I slip the robe over my breast and hasten out of the room.

The footsteps round the corner and the militant triumphantly points at me. "There she is!"

Next to him walks the delivery doctor.

"You can't take him away from me, he's mine!"

I run to the end of the hallway, to the large window. It's cracked open. I grab on to the frame and step on the hot radiator, hoisting myself up on the windowsill.

A door opposite the nursery opens and a woman's head sticks out. She looks for the source of the noise.

"Where the hell are you going?" says the militant.

"Somewhere where I don't have to see your ugly mug."

A couple patients gather up by the doctor and engage in fervent whispers.

"That's enough!" The militant strides to the window, a hand on his holster. "Get down, or—"

CHAPTER TWENTY-NINE

I push the windowpane open.

There is a collective intake of air and the militant stops, uncertain.

"Or what? You will shoot me? Go ahead. Is that all you can do?" I pass my eyes over the assembly. More post-labor women have gathered in the corridor in the meantime. They all stare at me, scared and curious. "Look at yourselves. You're animals caged by fear."

I grip Pavlik firmer.

"Do you want to hear me confess? Is that what you want?" I raise my voice. "Well, you won't get it because I'm not sorry! I would've killed him over and over! You want to accuse me of manslaughter, of committing a crime? But who are you to decide what's unlawful? What do you do, day in and day out? You lie and pretend and cheat and hide and you're afraid to speak your minds!"

The militant takes a step.

"Don't move!"

He halts.

I peer outside.

Moscow is waking. Seven or so stories below, cars bustle along the street; above it spreads out thick drab grayness. I look at Pavlik. "You still want to come with me?"

He studies me with dark trusting eyes and then he blinks once, as if he agrees.

"Okay."

I face them. "You think it's my end? You're wrong. It's my beginning."

The sky calls to me. My fingers lengthen into feathers. My robe falls off and gives way to a black shiny mantle with the white crown of a predator and—

The eagle perches on the edge of the sill. It waits for the eaglet, a ball of silver fuzz with tiny talons, to climb onto its back and grip its nape. The vobla flings itself at the birds. The eagle snatches it out of the air and tears at it with its beak and consumes it and screeches at the barking dog and the herd of cows, sending them to stampede away.

It turns around, clumsily, moving first one leg, and then the other.

The clouds are gone, burned away by the sun. It shines bright against the blue of the sky and the eagle thinks it looks like a golden city. The little eaglet trembles in fright, squeaks, sinks its talons deeper.

The eagle spreads its wings and takes off.

The ground below slants, falls back. Buildings blur in the bluish haze. Wind washes over the eagle's body and whistles in its ears and carries it upward. Exhilarated by the flight, it screams and dives and swoops down and passes so closely to the road, it startles a flock of ravens pecking at something in the ditch. They croak and scatter, abandoning their meal.

A dead jackal.

The eagle and the eaglet fly on.

ABOUT THE AUTHOR

Ksenia was born in Moscow, Russia, and came to US in 1998 not knowing English, having studied architecture and not dreaming that one day she'd be writing. Irkadura is her third novel. Her other books are Rosehead and Siren Suicides trilogy (which is really one book in three parts). She lives in Seattle with her boyfriend and their combined three kids in a house that they like to call The Loony Bin.

ABOUT THE BOOK

Irkadura was expertly edited by Colleen M. Albert, The Grammar Babe. Final formatting was completed by Stuart Whitmore of Crenel Publishing. Text is in Adobe Garamond Pro. Final digital assembly of the print edition was completed using Microsoft Word and Adobe Acrobat. The electronic edition was mastered in ePUB format using Sigil.

You finished it?
How many Buckets
of tears did you cry?
Please review it
(if you're alive)
and tell me what
you want to Read next
kseniaanske @gmael.com
СПАСИБО!
(Thank you!)

Note written by Lily
the Packaging Goddess
Instagram:
    @Basically-Matilda

Made in the USA
San Bernardino, CA
30 August 2017